GHOSTS NEVER DIE

ALSO BY JOEL A. SUTHERLAND

The Haunted series

The Nightmare Next Door

Field of Screams

Ghosts Never Die

Night of the Living Dolls

Ghosts
Never Die

Joel A. Sutherland

sourcebooks
young readers

Published by Sourcebooks Young Readers, an imprint of Sourcebooks Kids
P.O. Box 4410, Naperville, Illinois 60567-4410
(630) 961-3900
sourcebookskids.com

Originally published as *Kill Screen* in 2017 in Canada by Scholastic Canada Ltd.

Library of Congress Cataloging-in-Publication Data

Names: Sutherland, Joel A., author.
Title: Ghosts never die / Joel A. Sutherland.
Description: Naperville, Illinois : Sourcebooks Young Readers, [2020] |
  Series: [Haunted ; 3] | Audience: Ages 8. | Audience: Grades 4-6. |
  Summary: "A scary video game comes to life when Evie accidentally
  releases its ghost into our world!"-- Provided by publisher.
Identifiers: LCCN 2020018459 | (trade paperback)
Subjects: CYAC: Video games--Fiction. | Ghosts--Fiction. |
  Orphans--Fiction. | Horror stories.
Classification: LCC PZ7.1.S8825 Gho 2020 | DDC [Fic]--dc23
LC record available at https://lccn.loc.gov/2020018459

This product conforms to all applicable CPSC and CPSIA standards.

Source of Production: Sheridan Books, Chelsea, Michigan, United States
Date of Production: September 2020
Run Number: 5019833

Printed and bound in the United States of America.
SB 10 9 8 7 6 5 4 3 2

To Charles, Bronwen, and Fiona,
the three best kids
(and future pre-readers)
a dad could hope for.

CHAPTER 1

I LOOKED AT THE ABANDONED cabin in the woods and knew that if I entered, I would die.

But I had to try.

An ancient evil dwelled inside—a spirit from a time before time, a harvester of lost souls, a ghost of the Netherrealm.

The Wisp.

She was hiding somewhere in the cabin and refused to leave. That's what had brought me there. I'd already disposed of every single evil spirit she had summoned, and now I was there to kill her. And if I couldn't kill her, I would banish her back to the Netherrealm. And if I couldn't do that, I would die trying.

But the Wisp couldn't be killed, and she couldn't be banished, which left me with only one option.

I hadn't given up; I was simply being realistic.

Many had tried before me. All had failed.

This wasn't my first attempt to defeat the Wisp, either. Every time I'd faced her, I'd died. This would be my 109th attempt.

The full moon lit the cabin's roof and the gnarled trees that surrounded it. The forest, silent and still, was heavy with fog. There was no wind; there were no animals. It was like the entire world was holding its breath, tense and anxious, waiting for something bad to happen.

I checked the kill screen strapped to my left forearm. It registered anomalies in the electro-magnetic field in my vicinity as well as sudden dips in the temperature, invisible movement through the air, changes in the atmospheric pressure, and a dozen other potential sources of paranormal activity. Each and every dial, gauge, and meter on its sleek touch screen was going haywire. I wasn't surprised. It wasn't Casper the Friendly Ghost waiting for me in the dark, dank corners of the cabin.

"You got this, Evie," I whispered to myself. "This is it. This is the time."

I rolled my shoulders, cracked my neck, opened the door, and stepped into the darkness. The room smelled like death. Not the pungent tang of rotting corpses. It was an odd mix of wet earth, dying flowers, decomposing wood, rotting eggs, and, hiding beneath it all, the thick acrid smell of smoke and ash. At least, that's how I imagined the cabin's odor. My kill screen registered high levels of biological decay and sulfur in the air, so I knew my hunch wasn't too far off.

Despite the moon being so large and full, none

of its light streamed in through the windows. I tapped a button on the left temple of my glasses, and the world suddenly took on a bright green hue. They had a built-in night-vision function that worked similarly to military goggles, except my glasses revealed cold spots instead of heat.

No one had lived in the cabin for a long time. The walls were full of holes, the floor was covered in dust, debris, and dirt, and there was very little furniture. That's not to say that it was empty. Dark, sticky stains were splattered across the floorboards, bones stripped of flesh were piled in the room's corners, and bloody handprints covered the walls.

Before I took another step, I adjusted the earpiece in my right ear, which would allow me to hear any voice phenomena that would otherwise be too quiet to detect. Then I pulled the soulburner free from my thigh holster and powered it up. It had four different types of rounds that could kill most ghosts with a single shot: iron, salt, chalcedony, and a kinetic energy cell. But even with the soul-burner, I didn't feel prepared. I wasn't facing a run-of-the-mill revenant, phantasm, or poltergeist. But I couldn't let that stop me from trying. Maybe I'd learn something new about the Wisp this time—some weakness or flaw that would help me take her down.

Yeah, right. That's what I'd told myself each of the past 108 times I'd faced her, and I was no closer to beating her than the first time I'd entered the cabin.

I cast another look around the filthy room. Nothing was there to help me. One time the Wisp had been waiting in this first room as soon as I'd opened the door; I was dead before I knew what had happened. I never knew which one of the cabin's thirteen rooms she'd be in before I entered and searched the building. It was unnerving to say the least.

One down, twelve to go. I moved on to the second room, then the third, fourth, and fifth. I didn't bother pausing to examine the contents of each. I'd spent a lot of time in them before, and none of the objects I'd found—an old doll with a voice box, a rusty wheelchair, a human skull—had been useful in beating the Wisp.

I lingered a little longer in the sixth room, the bathroom. It was small and cramped—you could sit on the stained toilet and wash your hands in the sink at the same time. I turned on the tap. As always, a stream of sand poured out instead of water. I always thought that was weird, even for such a strange cabin. I put my hand under the steady stream, and the sand scattered across the floor.

I saw a brief blur of movement out of the corner of my eye, but when I spun around there was nothing there, just the wall. I had a feeling I knew where I'd find the Wisp. I turned off the tap and left the bathroom.

I entered the seventh room: the kitchen. The open fridge was filled with squirming maggots and skittering cockroaches. It looked like the garbage disposal had been used as a meat grinder, and the Wisp—

A ball of air caught in my throat, even though I was expecting to see her. I raised my soulburner and pointed it at her. She was hovering in the corner, a few feet off the ground.

The Wisp didn't flinch. She didn't even blink. She stared at me with glassy, black eyes. Her gaze made me feel like I'd been lulled into hypnosis. She was surrounded by a cloak of white fog that swirled around her. Her pale, smooth skin appeared to be made of a faintly glowing light blue mist.

She held her left hand palm-up in front of her chest, right where her heart would be if she had one. I'd never seen her move that hand before; on prior visits she always held it in the exact same place. Floating above her hand was an orb of bright yellow light that blurred the air, like the waves that radiate off asphalt on a hot summer day.

"I have come to send you back to the Netherrealm," I said. "You are an agent of darkness and are not welcome here among the living."

My voice echoed and boomed throughout the cabin. The last piece of high-tech ghost hunting gear I wore was permanently pierced in my tongue, a skull-shaped metal bead called a Ghost Box. But this was not simply a piece of jewelry—it was one of the most formidable pieces of equipment I owned. It contained an incredibly small but phenomenally powerful microphone that simultaneously cranked the volume of my voice and transmitted my words at exceptionally high frequencies heard only by spirits. Many times I'd just had to speak to make a ghost do what I wanted without needing to fight.

The Wisp merely laughed, softly and quietly. Silence followed.

I wondered if I could get two shots off before she killed me this time. None of the four types of ammunition had had any effect on her before.

But if I could combine two types—salt and an energy cell, maybe...

Her voice flowed into my ear, swirled around my mind, and rushed through my body like cold rain and firecrackers. "You are not worthy to live," she said without anger or hatred. The only hint of emotion I picked up in her tone was anticipation. "But you are worthy to die."

I practically mouthed the words with her. Her speech was always the same. So was what followed. The room grew darker, the Wisp glowed brighter, the air became heavy, her fog crackled with electricity, and then...

I died.

CHAPTER 2

I THREW MY WIRELESS VIDEO game controller across the basement in frustration, sat and stewed for a moment, and then rushed over and picked it up.

"I'm sorry," I told Toni, my controller, as I checked him for damage. I called him Toni after Toru Iwatani, the creator of *Pac-Man*, using the first and last two letters of his name. Toni looked okay. "I shouldn't take out my anger on you."

Toni was a limited-edition *Kill Screen* controller worth all the gift money I'd received on two separate birthdays and a Christmas. And yes, sometimes I talked to him, but that wasn't so weird. Plenty of hard-core gamers did the same. And besides, he had never talked back, so I knew I wasn't losing it.

"You know you're losing it, right, V?"

"I'm not," I told Harold with a sneer. He was my best friend despite what he thought of my behavior. I flopped down onto the couch beside Harold and took a big slurp of orange pop. "So don't even start."

"All righty, then." Harold looked at me like I was an alien.

"It's this game," I said in a whine, pointing at the video game console in frustration. "It's impossible to beat."

"Try not to beat yourself up," Harold said. *"Where There's a Will—"*

"There's a Wraith," I said, finishing *Kill Screen*'s tagline. "So cheesy."

"I noticed the bathroom glitch again."

"Yeah, me too." Sometimes, when the Wisp was in the kitchen, the left half of her body bled through the bathroom wall. It was one of many glitches in the game, and even though it gave me a heads-up on the Wisp's location, that had never helped me at all.

"Has anyone else beat the game yet?" Harold asked.

I shrugged. "Let's check."

The words **YOU'RE DEAD** floated around the screen in a cloud of mist above **PLAY AGAIN? YES/ NO.** I quit the game and turned on my phone. I kept a browser page open to the Grim Reapings website at all times. Grim Reapings was the indie video game company that created *Kill Screen*. The game became a massive international hit simply because no one had been able to defeat the end boss, the Wisp.

Word had spread that there was a poorly designed game on the market that was supposed to be impossible to beat, and sales skyrocketed.

The task of taking down the Wisp was like the quest for the Holy Grail, at least in gamer circles. Thanks to a steady diet of fantasy books and movies, geeks were hardwired to love a good challenge.

I'd bought a copy two months earlier during March break, and it felt like I wouldn't be able to rest until I beat the game. I'd been addicted to video games for a couple of years, but my addiction had reached new heights with *Kill Screen*. And something about the fact that Grim Reapings was located in Halifax, an hour's drive from my hometown of Wolfville, made me want to be the first to beat the game all the more.

I clicked on their message board, logged in with my username, "V," and scrolled through the most recent posts. "Nope, no one's beat it yet."

"So there's that," Harold said with an encouraging smile.

Good old Harold. We didn't have a lot in common. In fact, in most ways we were opposites.

He was a little on the short side and a bit round, while I was tall for my age and athletic. He rarely played video games, and while I might have been a gamer geek, I used to play on our school's soccer and basketball teams. He got really good grades, and I...not so much. Weirdest of all, he was a Trekkie and I was into *Star Wars*. Like I said, opposites.

But for most of my life our houses were side by side, and we'd grown up together. Other than my family, I'd spent more time with Harold than anyone else. He made me feel good about myself, and I often made him laugh—either with me or at me. So although we weren't identical, we were best friends. And he'd been there for me after the accident, when I'd needed him most.

I opened a message board thread I had started when I'd begun playing *Kill Screen* and quickly typed a new post: **ATTEMPT #109: DEAD.**

Other gamers had started similar threads of their own. I wasn't the only person who had come close to beating the Wisp, but I had reached her more times than anyone else. It wasn't only impossible to beat her; it was nearly impossible just to reach her cabin.

People started posting encouraging responses as soon as I'd published my comment, but since I was with Harold I didn't read them. I clicked some buttons on my controller and returned to the game's home screen. "You want to play a little multiplayer?"

"Nah. You'd mop the floor with me. I prefer watching you play."

"You sure?"

Harold nodded and rubbed his nose. "It's fun." I looked at him skeptically.

He raised his right hand as if taking some sort of oath. "I'm serious. You're going to beat the Wisp one of these days, V, and I want to be here when you do it."

"Thanks," I said, genuinely touched. I picked up the video game case and stared down the cover illustration of the Wisp. "Hear that? I'm coming for you, you and your weird glowing orb."

I dropped the case on the couch between us and Harold picked it up. "Her orb reminds me of something," he said quietly, more to himself than to me.

"What's that?"

Harold looked up. "Oh. Her orb—it looks like a will-o'-the-wisp."

"And that is...?"

"A soul that leads people off forest paths late at night, straight to their deaths." Harold shrugged and tossed the case on the coffee table. "I read about them on Wikipedia."

"You read too much Wikipedia."

"True," he said with a sheepish shrug. "You start on one page, which leads to another, and another... It's like falling down a rabbit hole. I also read that some people believe ghosts are made of untapped energy that can never be destroyed— even Einstein said something like that, I think. Don't quote me on that."

"Evie!" It was my grandmother, shouting down from the main floor. I still didn't think of it as my house, even though I'd lived there for two years. "Are you and your *boyfriend* still down there?"

She'd known Harold for years—he'd come over a few times a week since I'd moved in—and yet she still teased me about him being my boyfriend. "Grandma! That's gross. No offense," I said to Harold.

"None taken," Harold replied. "The feeling's mutual."

"Is he staying for dinner?" Grandma shouted. "I made mac 'n' cheese with cut-up hot dogs in it."

My favorite. "How can you say no to that?" I asked Harold.

"Like this: No." He looked at his watch. "Besides, I should go."

"Your loss." I faced the stairs and shouted, "He's not interested, Grandma. He wouldn't know fine dining if it bit him in the mouth, the tongue, *and* the stomach."

"If you eat a plate or two of mac 'n' cheese with hot dogs," Harold said, "it'll bite you in the stomach later on, I can promise you that."

I started to laugh as Harold rose from the couch to leave, but my head suddenly drained of blood, and I froze.

I'd spent the past three hours fighting pixelated ghosts. But now, hiding in the shadows across the room, stood a real one.

CHAPTER 3

I USHERED HAROLD OUT OF my grandmother's house more quickly than normal. I hoped he'd assume I was just really eager for dinner (a believable story considering the menu). I didn't think he had noticed the expression on my face when I'd looked over his shoulder and noticed what I'd seen in the corner. A dead woman with dark hair and dark eyes, staring at me from out of the shadows. A ghost.

They often came to me, sought me out—like,

on a nearly daily basis—with wide, pleading eyes and clawing hands.

I wasn't born with a sixth sense or anything like that. It had started two years earlier, after the accident. It was in the cemetery during my parents' funeral—there was an old man with a bushy gray beard and a tie-dyed shirt. He didn't even wait for my parents to be lowered into the ground before asking me to pass a message along to his son. I thought he was someone I didn't know; a grief-stricken stranger who had wandered over, but no one else at the funeral noticed him. And then he walked straight through one of my mom's cowork-ers, who was oblivious to the ghost's presence.

That's when I panicked. I started yelling and screaming at the old man to leave me alone. I took a few hurried steps backward, then tripped and fell. My grandmother helped me up and led me away. Everyone thought I was suffering some sort of trauma or shock from the deaths of my parents, but Tie-Dye—the ghost—followed us all the way to my grandmother's car and stood staring in at me through the window until we finally pulled away.

It wasn't until some time had passed that I realized Tie-Dye wasn't the first ghost I had ever seen. I had seen two the night before my parents died. If only I'd listened to them.

Nor was Tie-Dye the last ghost I saw. They continued to come to me like an army of ants whose hill had been kicked over, and they all had unfinished business they wanted me to take care of for them. As if it was my job to do all the stuff they never got around to doing before they croaked. I was in the eighth grade! I wished they'd just leave me alone.

But on the other hand, maybe one day I'd get to see my parents again. Maybe they'd even need some help, like the others. So I'd decided to assist the ghosts that came to me—as much as I could— even if it was a thankless, tiring, and occasionally creepy job.

At least the ghost in the basement was a woman in her twenties. The kid ghosts... They were the worst. How did you tell a five-year-old that they were dead and had to move along to wherever spirits go in the afterlife?

To the uninitiated eye, the dead woman would have looked alive. She was a little pale, sure, but some people just need more sun. And her skin glowed a bit, but that could have been a trick of the light. I'd gotten pretty good at picking out the dead from the living over the past two years. It was in their eyes. The whites were still white, but their irises were always black—never blue, brown, or green. And if you got close enough (I wouldn't recommend it) you'd see a small white dot flickering deep in their pupils.

What really freaked me out about this ghost wasn't how she looked. It wasn't her skin or her eyes. It wasn't even the fact that she'd appeared out of the shadows in Grandma's basement. I was used to all of that.

What freaked me out was what she said.

As I hurried Harold up the basement stairs, I heard her whisper over my shoulder.

"I'm here to help you."

CHAPTER 4

I'M HERE TO HELP YOU. Not *I need your help*, like every other ghost.

Her words swirled around my head as I pushed mac 'n' cheese around my plate with a fork. What did she mean, here to help me? No ghost had ever said anything like that before. What could she do for me? I shook my head and decided to put her out of my mind, comforted slightly by the knowledge that no ghost had ever approached me more than once. I'd helped out many over the years, but sometimes I had simply walked away. They might follow for a while, like Tie-Dye, but as soon as they were out of sight that was it—they were out of my life.

Like my parents.

"What's the matter, dear?" Grandma asked from across the kitchen table.

"Huh?" I said absentmindedly.

"I just told you I'm going to Halifax tomorrow and offered to give you and your boyfriend a ride, and you didn't even grunt in reply. Furthermore, I've never seen you take longer than three minutes to eat a plate of mac 'n' cheese and hot dogs." Her piercing eyes stared into my own. She was very young as far as grandmothers go—only sixty—but she had perfected the you-can't-fool-me grandma stare. "It's now been five minutes, and you've barely made a dent."

"First of all, for the millionth time, Harold isn't my boyfriend. And secondly, I guess I'm not hungry."

"I don't believe that. You're thinking about your parents, aren't you?"

I sighed and set my fork down. It made a dull *clunk* sound. I'd lied about not being hungry, but now my appetite actually was nearly gone. "I'm always thinking about my parents," I said quietly.

Grandma's face softened, and she offered a sympathetic smile. "Worrying and stressing about what happened won't bring them back. Focus on the positives—remember all the good times."

"Easier said than done."

"Fair enough." She reached across the table and patted the back of my hand. "But you and I both know they wouldn't want us to be sad, especially since it's been two years."

I'd found out during soccer practice. I'd never forget that day. How could I? Moments like that become a part of you, tightly and intricately woven into the threads that make you who you are.

I was running laps with my teammates when the school principal came out the back door and approached my coach. I was on the other side of the field, short of breath, cheeks burning, in the midst of a runner's high. I could see them talking, but couldn't hear the words. They stopped talking and scanned the track. As soon as their eyes locked on me I knew, with a sickening feeling in my gut, that something bad had happened.

There's one thing none of the pamphlets and books about grief tell you: When accidents kill someone you love, the accidents don't just happen to the victims. Those accidents happen to their loved ones, too. When Coach called me over and the principal told me what had happened, I felt like I'd been hit by the same truck that had hit my parents' car as they drove home from lunch that day, killing them both instantly.

The feeling didn't go away. I continued to feel like I was being hit by a truck every time I thought back to the "dream" I'd ignored the night before they had died. I had stayed up watching a late-night *Screamers* marathon on TV and fallen asleep on the couch. A series of nightmarish images filled my dreams—a haunted corn maze, a possessed doll, a killer horse—before I dreamt of my parents. They looked so lifeless, as if their bodies had been drained of blood, as if they were no longer in possession of their souls. Their skin was pale, their eyes were dark, their arms hung limp at their sides, and they spoke with no emotion.

"Help us," they whispered in unison.

My mother said, "Don't let us—"

"Drive," my father said.

"Don't let us—"

"Go," my mother finished.

I rubbed my face and looked at the clock. It was a little after three. The dream felt oddly real.

"Why?" I said, not considering why my subconscious mind had taken this odd turn.

"We will die," my father said.

"We are already dead," my mother added with finality.

"But you can help us," they said in unison once more, and then they both disappeared.

I rubbed my face again, which is when I assumed I'd woken up and stumbled up to bed, forgetting about my parents' warning by the time my head hit the pillow.

A week after the funeral, once I started to come out of my daze, I went online to find out if anyone else had ever experienced anything like what I had, because I'd decided that it hadn't been a dream. That's when I first read about crisis apparitions, ghosts of people who are still alive that appear to loved ones shortly before they die.

My parents told me they were going to die. They asked me to help them. And I didn't do anything.

I moved in with Grandma, and Coach told me to take all the time I needed—that I'd still have a spot on the team whenever I was ready to return. I never did.

Instead I retreated to the basement and hooked up the old gaming console my parents had given me for Christmas one year. I played all the games I'd collected when I was younger: *Mega Man*, *Super Mario Bros.*, *Donkey Kong*, *Tetris*, *The Legend of Zelda*. It was perfect. No one got hurt, and all I had to do any time I died was restart the game.

I felt better, but only for a while. The games were too basic, and I beat them all easily. I bought a newer console and a few games, then a few more, and a few more after that. The newer games were harder to beat, but no game took me longer than a week to complete. Every time I got a new game, I'd stay up late for a few nights in a row, sitting in the flickering blue light of the TV, staring at the screen like a zombie, mashing buttons until I'd beaten the game. And then I'd repeat the process with the next one I bought.

Simply put, I *had* to win—all the time. It distracted me, gave me purpose, kept me going, masked my feelings of guilt. Which is why I was so focused on beating the so-called unbeatable *Kill Screen*.

And maybe one day my parents would come back, and I'd be able to help them.

Grandma stopped patting my hand and leaned back in her chair. The cheese sauce was already beginning to stick to our plates. She took a bite. I took a small bite, too. It might not have looked great, but it still tasted all right. Before I knew it, I'd finished my first helping and had grabbed seconds. I asked Grandma if it would be okay if I took it upstairs so I could use my computer while I ate. I slipped a couple of salt-and-pepper packets into my pocket—Grandma always saved them from fast-food restaurants, proclaiming "Waste not, want not,"—and excused myself. By the time I reached the top of the stairs I was starting to feel more like myself again.

That changed the moment I stepped into my bedroom.

The ghost from the basement was waiting in the darkness for me.

CHAPTER 5

I FLINCHED AND JUMPED BACKWARD, shocked by the intrusion. Not because a ghost was there, per se, but because I'd never seen a ghost return once I'd left it. I steeled my nerve and turned on the light. It didn't make the ghost disappear or anything, but it did make me feel a little less creeped out.

"What do you want?" I asked, closing the door softly behind me and placing my plate on the computer desk.

The ghost's eyes were wide; her hair messy

and black. She didn't move. "I'm here to help you."

"So you said." Her directness didn't unnerve me at all. Most of the ghosts I'd dealt with were direct; it was like people's manners died with their bodies. And that suited me just fine. The sooner I could get rid of her, the better. "Help me how?"

She hesitated while her eyes darted around the room, as if she was stalling while trying to figure out how to proceed. "I know what you've done," she finally said.

"What I've done?" I asked, genuinely confused.

"You're getting too close," she continued.

A bad feeling surfaced in my gut. "I don't know what you're talking about."

She crossed the room toward me. "You are going to bring about our destruction." She crept closer and closer, passing through my bed instead of walking around it. "You will kill us all."

"Whoa. Hold on." I raised my hands but held

my ground. My temper was starting to flare. "I'm not going to kill anyone."

"Wrong," she said. "You have to stop. And if you don't promise to stop on your own, I'll make you." Her lips pulled back in a sneer, and the white lights in her black eyes danced madly.

Stop what? I wondered. My anger quickly gave way to fear. I felt blindly behind my back. I was pressed against my door—I could fling it open and make a run for it, but what would be the point? If this insane ghost really wanted to hurt me, she would catch up to me in a matter of seconds.

My pulse drummed in my ears. I could feel panic taking hold. Yet somehow an idea emerged.

What if the techniques that worked in *Kill Screen* also worked in the real world? Specifically, what if the soul-burner's ammunition was actually able to repel ghosts? Not iron, chalcedony, or energy—I didn't have any of those at my fingertips—but I had something else.

I reached into my pocket and pulled out one

of my grandmother's salt packets. In one swift motion, I tore the packet open and dashed the contents at her face.

It worked. The salt didn't hit her, but she screamed in alarm, flew across the room, and disappeared through my wall.

I stared at the empty salt packet in disbelief for a moment and then threw it in the trash. My sense of relief was short-lived. What if the ghost came back in the middle of the night while I was asleep? She was angry and out for revenge, a bad combination, and I'd be defenseless.

There were still two more salt packets in my pocket. I tore them both open and sprinkled the contents in a ring around my bed. Grandma wouldn't be thrilled if she found out I'd poured salt on the carpet, but that was better than being killed in my sleep by a ghost.

I turned out the light and slipped beneath the covers. For a while I replayed *Kill Screen*'s final level in my mind. I'd done this most nights in the months since I'd bought the game. I was looking for a clue or a hint, any small detail I'd possibly overlooked in the cabin that would be the key to defeating the Wisp. And that night, after the confrontation I'd just experienced, I needed a distraction.

But like every other night, I couldn't think of a thing. It was as if the game had been purposefully designed to be unbeatable. Or maybe there was some sort of glitch in its programming.

Unfortunately, my thoughts turned back to the ghost.

You are going to bring about our destruction, she had said. *You will kill us all.*

What a drama queen. Even if I wanted to single-handedly bring about the apocalypse, how would I go about doing that?

I dismissed the thought and closed my eyes. As I drifted off I pictured the ghost standing beside my bed in the dark, her black hair framing her pale white face and her dead eyes staring at me with fury. My final thought was that maybe that wasn't a dream—maybe she really was watching me right then...

And then I fell into a troubled sleep.

CHAPTER 6

IT WAS THE MIDDLE OF the night.

I sat up in bed and slipped my feet over the edge. They dangled there for a moment, hanging in the perfect spot for anything or anyone hiding under the bed to reach out and grab them.

I stood up and moved slowly across the room like a sleepwalker, leaving the safety of the salt ring.

Quietly, I snuck down to the basement and sat in my well-worn spot on the couch.

There was an odd sound coming from the walls, a mixture of a hum and a buzz.

A pungent smell that I couldn't quite place—something rotting—wafted under my nose.

I stared at the television screen in silence. Had I come down here to play a video game? Watch a late-night movie or an episode or two of *Screamers*?

I couldn't remember. My head felt foggy, and my mind was slow.

A small pinpoint of white light illuminated the center of the screen. Had I turned on the TV? I looked down at my right hand. I held the remote, but I honestly couldn't remember pushing the power button—I couldn't even remember picking it up. The white dot grew larger, slowly, a little larger, still slowly, bigger and bigger, but slow, slow, very slow.

I frowned and laughed in confusion, wondering what—

The ghost burst through the television screen

with an earsplitting crash. Glass shards flew in every direction. My body tensed, and my mouth opened in a silent scream.

The ghost, however, wasn't silent. She shrieked as she crawled out of the broken frame and reached for my throat. Her nails had turned into sharp claws and her skin looked paler than before.

"You'll kill us all, I'll kill you," she chanted in a bloodcurdling pitch. "You'll kill us all, I'll kill you! *You'll kill us all, I'll kill you!*"

She dug her fingers into the soft flesh of my neck and squeezed.

"No," I tried to say, but I couldn't say anything at all.

My pulse slowed, my heart stopped, my vision went black, and I woke up.

CHAPTER 7

THE NEXT MORNING, I FELT exhausted and sore, but I was thankful it was Sunday, and I could spend the day doing nothing.

I walked to the bathroom and splashed water on my face. I'd woken up once in the night from a bad dream, but it had already begun to fade from my memory.

After a quick shower and a bowl of cereal with Grandma, I texted Harold and asked him to come over. I grabbed Grandma's last salt packet (just in case), a box of Frosted Blue Raspberry Pop-Tarts, and a cream soda (second breakfast of champions) and went to the basement. He texted back as I tossed the salt and the food on the coffee table. I flopped down on the couch and fired up my video game console. Harold walked down the stairs twenty minutes later, just as I reached the Wisp's cabin.

"What's up?" I said as he took up his usual spot beside me. I was so engrossed in the game I hadn't even heard my grandmother let him in.

"What's up?" he replied.

I entered the cabin without pausing to check the readings on the kill screen strapped to my wrist or that my soul-burner was fully loaded and ready to rock 'n' roll. I'd reached this point in the game so many times that I knew it like the back of my hand. Plus, I also knew I'd most likely die a horrible, horrible death, so why prolong it?

"Get busy killing, or get busy dying," I said without meaning to speak out loud.

"Huh?" Harold said.

"Oh, um, it's from a book. Or a movie. I don't remember. I think I changed it a little." I entered the first room on the right. It was empty. I moved on.

"What's with you?"

"What do you mean?" I didn't take my eyes off the screen. The second and third rooms were also empty.

"You seem different."

I paused the game and turned to face Harold. So far he was the only person I'd ever told about seeing ghosts—I'd never even told Grandma. I wasn't sure if he believed me but he didn't question my sanity.

"A ghost visited me last night," I said. He didn't laugh or roll his eyes, so I told him the rest. How she didn't want help, but seemed to think she needed to help me. That she thought I was going to kill everyone. Blah, blah, blah... I made sure to emphasize how creepy she was, how she'd threatened me, and how I'd needed to sleep within a circle of salt so she wouldn't murder me in the night.

Harold kept a straight face through the entire story. Not much fazed him.

"Do you think," he said, "that the ghost might have told the truth? That you'll somehow bring about our destruction?"

"No way," I was quick to say. "That's nuts!" But the look on Harold's face was so serious and genuine that I was forced to reconsider. "Why? Do *you* think that's a possibility?"

He shrugged noncommittally. "I dunno. Why else would a ghost bother coming here to tell you that? And do ghosts have the ability to see the future, or something?" He shrugged again. "None of this makes sense."

"You can say that again," I replied. "No, I've never met a ghost that could see the future. Most are confused and aren't sure what's happening in the present. Many don't even know they're dead!" I grimaced, thinking back to the previous summer. "I once saw a decapitated ghost walking down Main Street, yelling at his own head for falling off. He held it in place on his shoulders and wondered aloud—and I'm not joking—if his doctor would have an opening to see him that day."

Harold laughed and shook his head. "I'm glad I never have to see stuff like that. I wouldn't be able to eat for a year."

I unwrapped a Pop-Tart and bit off a corner. "You get used to it," I said as I chewed noisily, crumbs flying out of my mouth with every word.

"You know, you eat really poorly for an athlete," Harold said.

"Ex-athlete," I corrected. I stuck the rest of the Pop-Tart in my mouth, picked up Toni and unpaused the game. "I won't make you stay. Feel free to leave if you're afraid of dying a horrible, tragic death."

Harold blew air noisily through his lips. "That's not going to happen."

"Your horrible, tragic death?"

"No, that's still a distinct possibility. I was referring to me leaving. If you're going to bring about our destruction, I want a front-row seat."

"It's your funeral," I said.

I searched a few more rooms in the Wisp's cabin but didn't find anything interesting.

"Do you think her warning is somehow connected to the fact that you can see ghosts?" Harold asked.

I shrugged. "Maybe. Maybe not."

"She said you're going to kill us all. Like, humans and ghosts. That's weird."

"Everything about her was weird."

As I continued to search the cabin with my mind on autopilot, I started to think back to the earlier levels of the game. What Harold had said got me thinking. The purpose of *Kill Screen* was to travel through a series of locations—both urban and rural—hunting ghosts and sending them all back to the Netherrealm using the

47

soul-burner. Each of the ghosts, including some incredibly nasty ones that appeared at the end of each level, had been summoned by the Wisp. She was some sort of supreme, ancient, all-powerful being that was dead set on killing everyone on the planet so that she'd be in charge of every spirit.

When you played the game, your character was the only person standing between the Wisp and the apocalypse.

I was close to beating the Wisp—I could feel it—but then that real-life ghost had appeared and told me that the apocalypse was coming and, somehow, it would be my fault.

I shook my head and shrugged. It was a small coincidence, that was all.

The Wisp appeared suddenly in a bedroom. "You are not worthy to live," she said, not even giving me time to recite the usual dialogue: that I'd come to send her back to the Netherrealm and she was an agent of darkness and all that stuff.

"But you are worthy to die," I said along with her.

Her eyes narrowed and darkened. The air thrummed with electricity. The orb that floated above her hand grew brighter—it looked like a bluish-white ball of fire.

And then, for the 110th time, I died.

Enough, I thought. *I will not die one hundred and eleven times. No way.*

But how? How could I beat an unbeatable end boss?

And then I had an idea.

CHAPTER 8

I ACTUALLY STARTED TO LAUGH. Yeah, like that peculiar person I had often promised Harold I wasn't.

But I didn't care how I sounded. I had an idea.

YOU DIED swirled around the screen like smoke from a snuffed candle.

"Something funny, weirdo?" Harold asked.

"Yeah, maybe," I replied, ignoring his joke. "What did you say the Wisp's orb reminded you of yesterday? Something you read about on Wikipedia?"

"A will-o'-the-wisp."

I nodded. "What if you're right? What if the orb is actually someone's soul? But it isn't there to lead people off the path. It is the path! The path to beating the Wisp."

For a moment Harold didn't look like he was buying it, but then his eyes suddenly widened, and he raised his fist to his mouth like he needed to bite down on something. He jumped off the couch, picked up the *Kill Screen* case from the coffee table, and pointed at the cover. "'Where there's a will, there's a wraith!' *Kill Screen*'s tagline!"

I could hardly believe it. Everything was starting to line up. "Of course! It's a hidden clue. The orb is literally a will-o'-the-wisp—a soul, or wraith, that she controls. Didn't you say that ghosts are energy? So if that's true, and the Wisp's orb is a will-o'-the-wisp, then maybe the orb is the source of her power, like a battery, and is the key to defeating her and winning the game." My mind was racing. "We need to find out how will-o'-the-wisps can be beaten."

Harold held up his free hand. His other hand was tapping furiously on his phone. "Way ahead of you."

"Let me guess: Wikipedia?"

"Uh-huh." His eyes darted left and right as he read quickly and muttered to himself. And then he smiled. "Got it! There are many variations of will-o'-the-wisps around the world, but all cultures seem to agree they're either ghosts or fairies seen in forests and swamps late at night. There's not a lot of talk about how to beat them—most sources simply warn people to avoid them and to never, ever follow them—but here it says that long ago in parts of Europe, Asia, and South America it was believed that if you could somehow catch a will-o'-the-wisp and submerge it, its flame would be extinguished and the soul would be released."

"That's it," I said. "It has to be. Now I just have to figure out how to soak the Wisp's orb."

"Any chance you can turn your soul-burner into a water gun?" Harold asked without much confidence.

"No, it can't be modified. It shoots salt, iron, chalcedony, and energy. That's it, that's all."

"Is there any water outside the cabin? Maybe a lake or a river you can lure the Wisp to?"

"Nothing I've ever seen, and the Wisp never leaves the cabin. She doesn't even leave whatever room she generates in with each new game."

"What about earlier levels? Did you ever see a water bottle or something you could add to your inventory?"

I shook my head. "I don't think so. But I guess I could start over and play through every single level and mission again, just to make sure." I sighed at the thought. How depressing. How boring. I took another bite of Pop-Tart and chewed robotically.

Harold claimed the last one from the box. He chewed, swallowed a mouthful, then sat up a little straighter. "What about the bathroom sink?"

"In the cabin? It didn't work, remember? No water."

"It didn't work the way you'd expect, but it did work. I mean, it's not like *nothing* came out when you turned on the tap."

"Yeah, but it was sand, not water. You said—"

"That to beat a will-o'-the-wisp you need to submerge it. The website didn't say it had to be water. And if the orb is anything like fire—"

"Sand would work, too!"

"It's worth a shot," he said, beaming. "But how do you get the sand out of the bathroom?"

I racked my brain but couldn't think how the game would allow me to collect the sand and carry it into a different room. When I put my hand under the stream of sand it scattered across the floor, but it wasn't a collectible item. "I don't know."

"Maybe you could replay the game until the Wisp is in the bathroom and throw some at her."

"Maybe, but whenever I enter a room the Wisp

kills me within a second or two. I won't have time to turn on the taps, let alone throw the sand at her."

We were close to figuring it out, closer than we'd ever been. This had to be the answer. It *had* to be.

I couldn't accept that the game was truly unbeatable.

"What if..." My mind was laying tracks of thought. I didn't quite know where the track might lead me, but the train started rolling nonetheless. "What if the Wisp didn't need to be in the bathroom, but somewhere else? What if... I entered the bathroom, alone, and then..."

It hit me.

"What?" Harold asked.

"OMG," I said, as I stood up slowly.

"What?" Harold shouted, standing with me.

"I might not be able to move the sand to a different room, and the Wisp might be too quick to be killed when she's in the bathroom, but none of that matters."

"I like where you're going with this."

"None of that matters," I repeated, "because there's a glitch in the game. I don't need to replay the game until the Wisp is in the bathroom. I need to replay the game until the Wisp is in the kitchen, beside the bathroom!"

"And then—"

"And then I throw the sand on her orb, the will-o'-the-wisp, when it accidentally appears through the wall."

"And then—"

I smiled at Harold. He smiled back at me. "And then no more Wisp."

CHAPTER 9

WE SAT BACK DOWN. HAROLD handed me Toni. I resumed the game.

The first stop was the bathroom. I watched the wall but the Wisp didn't come through it. Before leaving, I tested the faucet just to make sure it still worked, and sand poured out.

I left, found the Wisp, and died.

I told myself it might take all day, so I was caught off guard when, on the next try, I entered the bathroom and saw the Wisp's arm and leg bleeding through the wall. I actually jumped, which was weird since I'd spent so much time playing *Kill Screen* that I no longer even blinked when the hidden ghosts and spirits of earlier levels suddenly leapt out of the shadows. I was dead to the game's jump-scare tactics. But an elbow and a knee sticking through a bathroom wall had me on the verge of fainting.

"So," Harold said. He wiped his palms on his pants. "This is it."

"This is it," I replied. My throat felt raw and rough. I tipped my cream soda can to my lips but it was empty.

The clock on the wall went *tick-tock, tick-tock*.

The Wisp was floating up and down and side to side. Every now and again the edge of her orb was visible for a brief moment, but never her face. So I knew she couldn't see me. Her movement was graceful and hypnotic, following a predictable pattern.

I turned on the tap. Sand began to fill the sink.

My pulse quickened, and my heart sped up, like it was trying to pound its way through my chest.

I put my hand under the faucet. Sand scattered across the sink. Some scattered on the floor around my feet.

"V?" Harold said. He sounded far, far away. "What are you waiting for?"

Tick.

I watched the Wisp sway.

Tock.

I listened to the pitter-patter of a thousand grains of sand dancing on the floor.

Tick.

I had worked toward this moment for months.

Tock.

And here it was.

The orb came through the wall. I turned my hand, sending a stream of sand straight for it.

Time either sped up or slowed down. I don't really remember which, but what I do remember vividly is what happened once the sand hit the orb.

I'll never forget it.

The Wisp died. Not with a bang or with a whimper.

She died with a G. And then an H. And then another G and another H. And then F, G, P, Q, H, I, P, Q, followed by a bunch more letters and a whack of 1s and 0s. The game froze, and the random string of letters and numbers marched across the screen from right to left. When they reached the middle they stopped, flickered, and then disappeared.

The screen went black, and the console turned off with a loud electrical crack that was followed by a high-pitched whine that slowly faded away.

I didn't move, blink, or breathe until Harold broke the silence.

"Um, what just happened?"

"I think I beat *Kill Screen*," I said. "And in the process killed my television."

But the television wasn't dead. It turned itself back on, as did the console.

The same smoky font that floated around at the end of every game appeared. But instead of reading **YOU DIED**, it read **YOU WON**.

I had won. After hours and days and months spent playing the game no one could beat, I, Evie Vanstone, had won.

I couldn't believe it.

I took a picture of the screen with my phone. My hands were shaking so bad that the picture was blurry, but the words could still be made out.

But then the smoke shifted and the words changed. It no longer read **YOU WON**.

It now quietly proclaimed: **ALL WILL DIE**.

CHAPTER 10

"UH, V?" HAROLD ASKED. "WHAT'S that supposed to mean?"

All will die. Seemed pretty straightforward, but that wouldn't be an appropriate response. Instead I shook my head and said, "I'm not sure. Maybe it's a teaser for a sequel? Or some programmer's weird idea of a hidden joke?"

That had to be it. It was a harmless Easter egg. Video games were full of stuff like that.

But the ghost's warning suddenly ran

through my head: *You are going to bring about our destruction. You will kill us all.*

ALL WILL DIE continued to swirl around the screen in silence. Where were the end credits? Why wasn't the game resetting to the home screen? I hit a few buttons on Toni but nothing happened.

I stood up and crossed the room, then knelt in front of the TV.

"What are you doing?" Harold asked. He sounded concerned.

"I'm turning the console off," I said. "The game's frozen. Not surprising, since it glitched out when I beat the Wisp."

I said that partly to make Harold feel a little better, but mostly to make *myself* feel a little better. I knew it wasn't frozen—the words were still moving. I just couldn't sit there and stare at them any longer.

I took a deep breath and placed the tip of my forefinger on the power button.

As soon as my skin touched plastic—but before I had pressed the button—the words on-screen faded away. I pulled my hand back and stared at the TV. Before long a string of bizarre characters and symbols appeared.

"You recognize this language?" I asked. "Doesn't look like anything I've ever seen."

"Me neither." The words were a weird mix of rounded, flowing characters and jagged lines that looked more like slash marks than letters. They looked *angry*.

The bizarre language slowly morphed into letters I recognized.

I read the words aloud. *"Slith sekae, slith hasei. Kahorra meen, vokalai skanda ilk hokuun. Kalaharra, tanzinae. Exat."*

The lights in the basement dimmed. The temperature plummeted low enough that we could see our breath as it puffed out of our mouths in thick, white clouds. Frost spread in spiderweb patterns across the small windows near the ceiling. The walls started to shake. The air started to thrum. It was hard to breathe. My heart felt like it was struggling to beat, like it had been trapped in a too-small jar. My head ached, and my skin crawled. I bent over at the waist, put my hands to my temples, and moaned. It didn't help.

Then I looked up.

Hovering a foot off the floor, between me and the television, was a ghost. Not the ghost from the day before.

The Wisp.

CHAPTER 11

"WHO HAS SUMMONED ME?"

The Wisp spoke with a mixture of grace and venom, somehow sounding bored and excited, quiet and forceful. She looked just like she did in the game, with bluish-white skin that glowed faintly and black glassy eyes.

Also true to the game, she held her left hand palm-up in front of her chest, and above it floated her golden orb. In person it looked like a glass ball that had trapped a solar flare.

Without the constraints that come with being pixelated, the mist that enveloped her from head to toe swirled slowly and hypnotically, as vivid and earthy as early morning fog. She smelled like a springtime forest, too, with underlying notes of wet stone, rotting mulch, and wood smoke. Like the mist, her odor was something the game couldn't accurately capture.

I tried to swallow, but my mouth was dry. "Um..." I said in response to her question. Not my most eloquent opening, but it wasn't every day I spoke to the ruler of the Netherrealm. "If beating *Kill Screen* summoned you, then that would be, uh, me." I raised my hand like a kindergartner in need of a potty break, then, feeling silly, quickly lowered it.

"I'm Evie Vanstone," I added, and then immediately winced. *Stop it*, I warned myself. *Don't reveal anything else.*

The Wisp regarded me with cool detachment and a twinge of amusement, or maybe disbelief.

I'm not sure. It was nearly impossible to guess what she was thinking.

"Thank you, Evie Vanstone," she said. "You are a friend of the Netherrealm."

A friend of the Netherrealm? No, no, no. She had the wrong girl. The dialogue my character had said almost every time I'd faced the Wisp in the game—*I have come to send you back to the Netherrealm*—rang through my head. The Wisp seemed to think I was on her side, that I'd summoned her on purpose. But I suppose the real Wisp wouldn't know that she'd killed me 112 times, or that I'd killed her once. She didn't know that we were enemies.

I nearly told her. I nearly shouted, "You are an agent of darkness and are not welcome here among the living!" But I stopped myself. She could probably kill me and Harold with a single snap of her fingers.

"Yes," I said with a low bow. I caught a glimpse of Harold. He looked confused, so I winked at him to let him know it was an act. "I, um, love the Netherrealm. It's my favorite place in the world. Or should I say in the underworld? I've never actually been."

"All in good time," the Wisp said. A thin smile flashed across her lips, briefly revealing teeth too sharp. "Remember that you have to die."

My gut clenched, and I dug my fingernails into the palms of my hand to stop from throwing up.

"*Everyone* will soon die," the Wisp added. The fog began to swirl more quickly around her, and she rose higher into the air. "We will meet again, Evie."

I nodded. I couldn't manage much else.

The Wisp turned and passed through the wall behind the TV, a trail of mist following her. Just before she disappeared, I could've sworn I heard a muted shriek come from the orb.

I took a deep breath as soon as she was gone. It felt like I hadn't breathed properly since she'd appeared.

"What," Harold said behind me, "was that?"

"That," I responded, "was the Wisp."

"Not what I meant."

"Yeah, I know," I said quietly with a nod.

Harold shook his head in disbelief and slowly exhaled. "Do you think *Kill Screen* was purposefully designed to be unbeatable, to try to prevent the Wisp from getting out?"

I shrugged. The thought made me feel sick. Had I done something I wasn't supposed to do?

That was a stupid question. *Of course* I had done something I wasn't supposed to do.

Harold continued. "Well, it could've been worse."

"How could it have been worse?"

"The Wisp could've killed us. I bet she *would've* killed us if you two weren't BFFs."

"We are not BFFs," I said, my mood lightening a little as my heart rate began to return to normal. "And yeah, it could've been worse. But now the Wisp is out there, doing whatever it is wisps do."

"Do you think..." Harold trailed off, swallowed, then continued. "Do you think this is what the ghost meant when she said you're going to kill us all?"

"Yes," I answered without hesitation or doubt. "Yes, I do."

"The end of the world..."

"And it's all my fault."

"So, what do we do about it?"

I sighed. I didn't know. Clearly we had to do *something*. But what? "If we tell your parents or my grandma, they'll think we're nuts. If we go to the police, they'll think we're nuts. If we try to warn the media, they'll think we're nuts. See a pattern here?"

"We can't just sit here and do nothing!"

I agreed with Harold, but I didn't have the chance to tell him that.

The ghost from yesterday flew through the wall.

"What have you done?" she screamed. Her eyes were wild. "I warned you. I warned you!"

In the blink of an eye, she was in my face, and her long, pale hands were squeezing my neck.

I couldn't breathe. Stars exploded before my eyes. And then, as quickly as flipping off a light switch, blackness.

CHAPTER 12

I WOKE UP.

I was lying in the middle of the floor, right where the ghost had attacked me. I couldn't tell how much time had passed, but it didn't feel like I'd been out for long. Maybe only a minute or two. Maybe less.

Harold was kneeling beside me, a look of worry on his face.

"Oh, V, you're okay," he said in relief. "Your face—it turned blue nearly as soon as the ghost laid hands on you. I've never seen anything like it."

I sat up and rubbed my pounding head gingerly. "What happened? Where is she?"

Harold pointed at the corner of the basement.

The ghost was skulking in the shadows and watching us with a mixture of hatred and concern.

"You can see her?" I asked Harold.

Harold nodded. Maybe ghosts could control who saw them and who couldn't, and when. "Don't worry," Harold said. "She flew off you as soon as I tore this open." He held up the salt packet I had brought down earlier in the morning. "And she doesn't seem too eager to come any closer now that she knows what I have."

"Thank you," I whispered to Harold. He smiled, blushed, and nodded.

"You have killed us all!" the ghost wailed. "The Wisp only has one purpose, one goal: to kill every human and reap every soul. And you," she pointed a shaking finger at my chest. "You released her."

"I didn't mean to," I said defensively. "All I did was beat a video game. And the last time I checked, beating a video game never killed anyone." I paused and considered something. "How did you know that beating *Kill Screen* would release the Wisp?"

The ghost retreated a little. She ran her fingers through her black hair and then rubbed her forearms.

Finally she said, "My name is Leda." She spoke so quietly I had to strain to hear her. "And I..." She trailed off, then restarted. "I worked for Grim Reapings. I was a game designer. I created *Kill Screen*."

It was one of those moments when time didn't just feel like it had slowed down—it felt like it had stopped. Like, dead in its tracks.

I stared at the ghost—at Leda—as her words sunk in.

"How did you know I was so close to beating *Kill Screen*?" I blurted out. Not the most tactful approach, but my head was quickly filling with questions, and I felt like my brain would explode in another second or two.

Leda didn't leave, and I took that as a good sign. "I can control electronic devices—phones, computers, tablets. I can fry them, too, if I want. I don't even need to physically touch them. I don't fully understand it—I don't think I've been dead long. But after I died, I saw your posts on the Grim Reapings website, so I came here and watched you. Once I knew you were telling the truth on the message board and were close to beating the game, I panicked and tried to stop you."

"Why didn't you just tell me what would happen? Why did you try to freak me out last night?"

Leda shook her head and rubbed her face, looking genuinely confused. "I don't know what came over me. I shouldn't have done that. It was a mistake."

I hadn't yet met a ghost that was completely rational, so I bought her excuse. "You said you haven't been dead long. When did you die?"

"I'm not sure," Leda said. "Not exactly. Time is difficult to keep track of. It's fast, it's slow. It doesn't follow a straight path like it used to. Maybe a week? Maybe a year?"

Harold googled "leda grim reapings" on his phone. "You were the victim of a hit-and-run in Halifax. The driver fled the scene. It was November first, the day after *Kill Screen* was released. Bad timing." Harold looked up quickly and his cheeks flushed. "Sorry. I didn't mean to make light of your death."

"It's okay," Leda said, but she looked depressed.

"I'm sorry, Leda," I said. "I know you're confused and upset, but why did you design *Kill Screen* to release the Wisp if you knew what she'd do?"

She broke eye contact and shook her head. "I don't remember."

"You remembered that she'd be released when

the game was beat and what she plans on doing now that she's free—" I paused and took a deep breath to calm my nerves (it didn't work) before continuing. "But you don't remember why you made it possible?"

"No, I'm sorry, but I don't."

I sighed. "How about how to beat her? Or even where she'll go? Do you have any guesses?"

Leda looked away and shook her head. She looked as guilty as I felt. Like it or not, we were in this together. But Harold—Harold didn't have to be involved any further.

"If you'd rather head home now, Harold, I totally understand," I said.

Harold looked like he might throw up at any moment, but he managed to shake his head. "No. I'm with you, V."

I forced a smile and nodded. "So, Leda, do you have any ideas how to jog your memory?"

To my surprise, she did. "Yes. One. But you're not going to like it."

"Why not?"

"We have to go to Halifax, to my office."

"Why wouldn't I like that?" Grandma had already offered to take me into the city, and I'd wanted to visit Grim Reapings since I'd become obsessed with *Kill Screen*.

"I've been using your phones to monitor social media sites the whole time we've been talking," Leda said.

I felt violated, somehow. Not that I had anything too private on my phone, but still, it was my phone.

Leda continued. "'Hashtag Halifax fog' is trending. I think the Wisp has beaten us there."

CHAPTER 13

AS WE DROVE ALONG THE highway from Wolfville to Halifax, I took stock of how surreal the past twenty-four hours had been.

A ghost had warned me that I was going to kill everyone. I had ignored the ghost and beaten an unbeatable game. Some sort of terrible, powerful, ancient spirit was released into the world. And now I was headed to the city with the ghost and my best friend to look for clues in the Grim Reapings office to beat said evil spirit.

It was like the storyline of a really weird video game, but without a cool soundtrack and the ability to pause or restart the game if anything bad happened to us. Oh, and my grandmother was driving us to face off against the end boss, completely unaware that anything out of the ordinary was taking place.

Grandma clearly couldn't see Leda, since she hadn't totally freaked out.

With his head resting against the window, and a faraway look in his eyes, Harold looked a little queasy.

"You okay?" Grandma asked Harold as she glanced at him in the rearview mirror.

"I'm fine," he said meekly. He glanced at Leda briefly and groaned, as if he still couldn't believe he could see her. "I get carsick, that's all."

"Don't worry about him," I told Grandma. Not because I didn't care about Harold, but because I wanted Grandma to focus on the road. The closer we got to Halifax, the fog's thickness made it impossible to see.

We took an exit near Bedford. Halifax—and whatever horrors awaited us there—were only fifteen minutes away.

~⟳~

"This. Is. Awesome."

Leda, Harold, and I were standing in the front lobby of the Grim Reapings offices, an old stone building on Lower Water Street near the Maritime Museum of the Atlantic. Leda had led us there after we'd split up from Grandma. I had asked Grandma if she wanted us to stay with her, and she replied that kids our age wouldn't want to be saddled with her on a Sunday afternoon. So we agreed to meet at the Split Crow at five o'clock for dinner. Although Leda doubted anyone would be working in her office on a Sunday, she wanted to make sure. We waited outside in the fog and listened to passersby talking about how unseasonable the weather was. Once Leda was certain the building was empty, she unlocked the door and let us in.

I stood statue-still and soaked it all in, finding it hard to believe that I'd gone from being just another kid trying to beat *Kill Screen* to a kid standing in the Grim Reapings offices.

"Really?" Harold said. "What about it, exactly, is awesome?"

"Everything," I said in awe.

Harold scanned the lobby and looked confused. "All I see is a desk, some doors, four plain walls, three posters..."

"I know," I said. "Isn't it great?" I pointed at the first poster on my left, which featured a white unicorn with a rainbow horn. "*Rainbow Crayon Unicorn.* The first game from Grim Reapings. The evil dragon Smog has polluted the world by covering it in a gray cloud that has sucked up all the color, so you have to use Rainbow Crayon

Unicorn's horn to color everything back in. It was a complete failure, probably because three-year-olds don't play video games much and—shocker—teens and adults weren't interested."

"Very few people even know what *Rainbow Crayon Unicorn* is," Leda said with a mixture of wonder and embarrassment. "I'd been meaning to take that poster down for months."

I smiled and pointed at the second poster, which showed a cartoon shark swimming straight up to the surface of a lake, where a bunch of monkeys were having a good time. *"Sharkey Shark and the Monkey Munch.* The second game from Grim Reapings. Underrated, in my opinion."

Now it was Leda's turn to look confused. "Thank you?" she said, half statement, half question.

"You play as Sharkey Shark," I continued, "and you, well, you munch monkeys. That's it, really. Pretty simple. But addictive. It was another total disaster. And then, of course, came *Kill Screen*." I pointed at the final poster on the wall.

The computerized Wisp stared back at us, menace in her pixelated eyes. A chill spread through my body, and I remembered the reason we were there.

Where there's a will, there's a wraith.

"We should carry on," I said. I checked my phone. It was nearly noon. Not knowing exactly where the Wisp was or what she was doing was worse than anything I could imagine.

Leda's office looked like a crime scene. Stacks of paper, notepads, and books covered every surface. Sticky notes with handwritten scribbles surrounded her computer monitor. Sketches from *Kill Screen* and what I assumed to be other games in development were taped one over the other on a large whiteboard mounted on the wall.

My first thought was that someone had ransacked the place after her death. But when I asked her, Leda shook her head.

"No, I was always just very busy. It may look chaotic, but I had a system. I always knew exactly where everything was. Luckily it doesn't look like any of my colleagues have been in here since I died."

"Okay, fine," Harold said. "So where's the clue you were hoping to find that might help you remember anything important?"

Leda shook her head. "I don't remember. Like I said, I've been confused."

"Well, let's start searching," I said.

We began digging through Leda's paperwork and rooting through her desk drawers. Before long I found a very small notebook, labeled THE WISP, on a bookshelf.

"Bingo," I said, and the others crowded in close and looked over my shoulders.

"My notebook!" Leda said. "I did a lot of research on the Wisp when I first started brainstorming about *Kill Screen*. I wanted the game to include as many real ghosts as possible." She took the notebook from me and opened it to the first page. "I remember... I read about the Wisp on some internet message board but couldn't find much else online. So I hacked into the website and found a secret encrypted members-only page. That's where I found most of this info."

"What was the name of the website?" Harold asked, turning on his phone and opening an internet browser.

Leda considered the question for a while but ultimately shook her head. "I don't know. Something with a couple of Ms."

"Monkey munch?" Harold asked with a smile. Leda didn't laugh.

An earsplitting *boom* thundered in my ears and shook the office windows. I shielded my head and dove under Leda's desk, certain we were under attack—certain that the apocalypse had begun.

CHAPTER 19

WITH EYES SHUT TIGHT AND hands over my ears, I waited for the sound of bloodcurdling screams to begin on the busy streets outside the office. I pictured the Wisp flying through the air with a scythe in hand cutting people down where they stood and harvesting their souls.

But nothing happened.

The boom that had sent me diving for cover was followed by silence.

I dropped my hands, opened my eyes, and

looked out from under the desk. Harold and Leda were staring back at me. Not only had neither of them dropped to the floor, but neither looked concerned in the slightest.

Heat flushed my cheeks. I got back to my feet. "You guys heard that, right?"

"Yeah, I heard it," Harold said.

"And it didn't even make you jump?"

"Of course not. It was just the firing of the noon gun." Harold looked at me skeptically. "You have been to Halifax before, right?"

"Yes, I have been to Halifax before," I said a little irritably. "You know I have, but I guess I've only ever been here later in the day because *that*—" I pointed out the window. "I would've remembered that."

Harold and I had gone on a school field trip to Fort George on Citadel Hill. Now that I thought of it, I vaguely remembered a tour guide at the fort saying they fired a cannon every day at noon.

"I worked here for years and never got used to it," Leda said.

That made me feel a little less embarrassed. "Leda, can I see that again?" I pointed at the notebook I'd found, eager to change the topic and get back on track.

She nodded and handed it over.

I flipped through the notebook. Jumbled notes were scribbled across the pages, making it hard to understand, but a few sentences jumped out at me.

> Like the Grim Reaper, the Wisp cannot kill.

That was good to hear.

> Her main pursuit is the death of all living humans and the enslavement of all souls.

That, not so much.

"Remember that you have to die."

I held the book open to Leda and tapped that quote. "The Wisp said this to me before she left the basement. You wrote it here in quotation marks. Do you remember why?"

"It was a memento!" Leda blurted out.

"A memento?"

"I think so." Leda's brow furrowed and she tapped her chin. "Sorry. That doesn't make sense, does it? How can an expression be a memento? I don't know why I said that."

"Maybe it was an expression printed or engraved on a memento?" I offered.

"Maybe," Leda said, but she didn't look convinced.

"Hmm..." Harold said. He was sitting at Leda's desk, flipping through a small black book.

"What's up, Harold?" I asked.

"Huh?" He jerked his head up as if he'd forgotten we were there. "Oh. I found your day planner." He pointed at November 1. "Your only appointment on the day you were hit by the car was with a man named Morrie."

"Morrie?" Leda said. "That is my handwriting, but I don't remember anyone named Morrie."

"Well, according to your schedule, you met with him at nine forty-five a.m." Harold flipped back through the pages. "That's the only time I see his name."

Leda looked more confused than before.

"Is Morrie a nickname for Maurice, or maybe Morris?" I asked.

"No, I don't think so. This is so frustrating. I always had such a good memory, I..." Leda trailed off. Her mouth dropped open and her eyes widened. She froze in silent contemplation.

"What is it?" I asked.

"Not Morrie. Mori. And Memento." One corner of Leda's mouth curled up slightly. It wasn't quite a smile, but it was the closest I'd seen her to looking happy. "Memento Mori!"

"Memento Mori?" I said, then turned to Harold. Before I could ask him to Google it, he said, "Already on it." A short moment later, he looked up from his screen and said, "It's Latin for 'remember that you have to die.' In Ancient Rome, slaves were assigned to follow victorious generals who'd returned from battle to remind them that they were mortal and would die one day. Apparently, it kept them from getting too big a head. Now, mementos mori are objects and artworks that remind people of their mortality— lots of skulls, basically."

"That's it," Leda said. "It's coming back to me."

"What else?" I asked.

Leda scrunched up her face and continued to think.

"Keep searching," I told Harold.

He scrolled through websites until one caught his attention. "Some people think there's a secret society called Memento Mori. I can't find much info on them—"

"Because they're secret," I quipped.

Harold continued talking without acknowledging me. "But conspiracy theorists believe Memento Mori members are interested in paranormal activity and the afterlife, and have chapters across the country."

While still facing Harold, I said, "Any of that ringing a bell, Leda?"

She didn't answer.

I turned. Harold looked up. Leda was gone.

CHAPTER 15

"WHERE DID SHE GO?" HAROLD asked.

"I don't know," I said. "You mentioned the secret society, and then she just...*poof.*"

"She's got an annoying habit of disappearing."

"No kidding. But she is a ghost, after all."

Harold sighed. "So what do we do now?"

"We could try to find her." I looked out the window. The street was still filled with thick fog, making it impossible to see more than nine or ten feet in any direction. "But where would we even start to look?"

"Even without Leda's help, we have to try to stop the Wisp."

"But we have no idea where she is, either."

"Let's work backward," Harold suggested.

"What does the Wisp want to achieve?"

I held up Leda's notebook. "According to this and what Leda has told us, she wants to kill every single human on the planet and enslave our souls."

Harold blinked and ran his fingers through his hair. "That's ambitious."

"The good news is she can't kill people herself. So, there's that."

"That's weird. The Wisp killed you every time—well, every time except for the last time—you reached her in the game." Harold was silent for a moment, then shrugged and added, "Anyway, how will she kill us all if she can't, you know, kill us all?"

I gave it a little thought. "She's going to need help."

"Like in..."

"Like in *Kill Screen*." I didn't want it to be true, but it was what it was. "She's going to amass an army of the dead."

"Of course," Harold said quietly. "And she'll use the ghosts to do her bidding. She'll have them kill everyone."

I nodded. "We'll be lucky if the Wisp in the game is similar to the Wisp in real life."

"Why?"

"Because then we'll know how to beat her. I've done it once, and I can do it again."

Harold snapped his fingers and smiled. "We submerge the Wisp's orb in water or sand."

"But first, we have to figure out where the Wisp is."

"Leda said she found most of her info about the Wisp by hacking into a website, probably Memento Mori's," Harold said. "Too bad we can't do the same."

"We don't need to." I held up the notebook.

"Leda already did that for us, remember?" I flipped through the pages again and scanned the handwriting while Harold peered over my shoulder. About two-thirds of the way through, he told me to stop and pointed at the top of the page.

Wisp: stuck in the Netherrealm (lucky for us!), but can be summoned. Maybe? Do more research!

Saancticae: ancient, forgotten language. A Saancticae chant must be spoken aloud to summon her. Look for such a chant—could be fun to add to game (authentic)!

I had read the words out loud at the end of the game. Me. Add that to the list of reasons I was ultimately responsible for the mess the world was in.

Other ghosts of the Netherrealm can be summoned by

- séances
- mediumship
- channeling
- using Ouija boards, crystal balls, mirrors, candles, spirit trumpets, spirit slates, and spirit cabinets
- countless other ways

Location of the summoning is important for success! Ghosts can only return through a location of personal significance (grave, or location of their death). But summoned spirits can bring others with it.

—I can use this in *Kill Screen*! (Wisp summons one or two evil ghosts, who then bring others with them, providing plenty of ghosts to beat in each level.)

Not all Netherrealm ghosts are evil.

Some are good and fight to prevent evil spirits from returning. Most souls pass on beyond the Netherrealm to places unknown, never to return.

I turned the page and read the next paragraph, but abruptly closed the notebook and slipped it into one of the pockets of my cargo pants.

"Hey," Harold said, looking at me in confusion. "Why'd you do that?"

Leda had written that if anyone ever managed to summon the Wisp, they would be given a position of power at her side in the Netherrealm. And if they refused, they would be destined for an eternity of pain and suffering...as would their friends and family, everyone close to them.

I tried to think of an excuse for why I closed the notebook when one suddenly appeared. I pointed at the window and said, "Look."

Sunlight poured through. The mist had cleared from the street. It had drifted up the hill to the west and swirled around Fort George on Citadel Hill.

"I think we now know where the Wisp is," I said.

CHAPTER 16

WE CAME UP WITH A plan as we walked. First of all, we needed salt, as much as we could carry. I tried to ignore the fog as we entered Pete's Fine Foods. We went straight to the baking and spices aisle. "We should keep our hands as free as possible," I said. "Take as many boxes of salt as you can carry in one bag." I tried sliding a box into one of my cargo pants pockets—it just barely fit. "Plus one for good measure."

Harold opened the metal spout on the side of

one of the boxes. "I like this. It'll be much easier to shake on ghosts than salt packets."

I glanced down the aisle and realized we weren't alone. A woman and her preschooler stared at us in bewilderment. They had obviously heard what Harold had just said.

My cheeks grew hot, and I blurted out the first excuse I could think of. "It's for a...school project. We're making a...student video." It might have been more believable if I hadn't paused to think of what to say next.

"A *Ghostbusters* spoof," Harold added, not exactly improving the situation. And then, just when I thought he couldn't make it any worse, he added, "Who ya gonna call?"

The woman shook her head, grabbed her son's hand, and quickly pulled him away.

"Just trying to keep you all safe," I said under my breath, too quietly for either of them to hear.

We paid for the salt—including the box in my pocket—and stepped back out onto the street. We didn't have kill screens strapped to our forearms, earpieces to hear paranormal activity, or tongue piercings to amplify our voices and help make ghosts follow our commands. We each had a bag full of table salt. It was the best we could do.

As we walked north on Dresden Row, the road grew congested with people, most of whom were staring up at Citadel Hill. When we got closer to the crowd, I realized the majority of the people were ghosts. Light blue glow, pallid skin, dead eyes...the works.

"You seeing this?" I asked Harold.

"The fog on the hill?"

"No, the dead people *staring* at the fog on the hill."

A couple of teenage girls suddenly stopped in front of us.

"Super weird, right?" one said to the other. "*Super* weird!" the second teen confirmed with excitement.

"Selfie!" they exclaimed in unison, then

turned their backs to the fog, held up a phone, made faces (one pretended to look shocked, the other made a duck face), took a few pics, laughed, and continued down the street. They walked right through a ghost, completely unaware that they had briefly passed through someone's soul.

"Were those two girls ghosts?" Harold asked. I shook my head.

"Then no, I don't see any dead people staring at the fog on the hill."

It made sense that only I could see them. Harold could see Leda, but she'd chosen to be visible to him.

The ghosts in the street were confused, anxious, and more than a little afraid.

I could relate. I felt the same.

"What is going on?" one of the ghosts asked me as we passed. He was an old man with a gray beard and a colorful shirt...

Tie-Dye.

"You're still here," I said with a mix of wonder

and sadness. I couldn't believe he hadn't passed on, well, *anywhere* yet.

Tie-Dye ignored the comment and pointed at the fog on Citadel Hill. "I don't like that."

The other ghosts within hearing distance muttered in agreement.

Tie-Dye turned and looked at me for the first time. He frowned for a moment before a look of recognition appeared on his wrinkled face. "You," he said, and some of his concern washed away. "I know you. You're the girl who can see us."

The other ghosts crowded around and looked at me with hope.

"Do you know what's happening up there?" Tie-Dye asked.

I nodded.

"It's bad, isn't it?"

I nodded again.

"Can you stop it?"

I paused. I didn't know what else to do, so I nodded one more time.

"Thank you," he said, and the others smiled, sighed in relief, and clasped my hands.

I knew they meant well, but their confidence made me feel a little sick to my stomach.

I broke through the ring of ghosts and beckoned for Harold to follow. Once we were out of the ghosts' earshot, he said, "You just talked to a bunch of dead people, didn't you?"

"Uh-huh," I said, my nausea increasing. Because, after what I'd read in Leda's notebook, I no longer felt so confident. So I'd lied to the ghosts. I was making a habit of lying to give people false hope and assurance. First Harold, then Tie-Dye and the others. If only I could lie to myself.

CHAPTER 17

WE CROSSED SACKVILLE STREET, BEGAN to climb the hill, and entered the fog.

A cold feeling washed over me, and a chill in the air turned my breath into puffs of soft frost. With every step my anxiety grew, and it felt like I was walking underwater. The Pete's Fine Foods plastic bag I carried got heavier and heavier. It was unnaturally quiet—even our footfalls sounded muted. But the worst part was that I couldn't see more than a few feet in any direction. At least we didn't have far to go. We knew the fort was dead ahead.

A small white rectangular building suddenly appeared ahead of us. It had three white tiers above the main floor, resembling a wedding cake. The first tier had only windows, the second had a large clock face on all four sides with narrow windows in between, and the third tier housed large bells. On top was a green dome.

"Old Town Clock," Harold said.

"Huh," I said.

"You shouldn't have come here," a voice whispered behind us.

Harold and I jumped. It was Leda.

"You scared us," Harold scolded. "Why'd you disappear earlier?"

I had a feeling I knew why, but I waited to hear her answer.

"I panicked," she said quietly. "I'm ashamed."

"Of what?" Harold asked.

She didn't make eye contact with us. "This is

all my fault. How could I have forgotten what I'd done?"

Harold looked at me. I looked away. He turned back to Leda. "What did you do?"

"It came back to me as I started to read my old notebook. As I said, I was researching the Wisp for *Kill Screen*. I found Memento Mori's website and hacked into it. The stuff I read there—about ghosts and the afterlife, the Wisp and the Netherrealm—it was weird and bizarre and more than a little freaky. What was even weirder at the time was that people believed in it all!" She laughed once, but the sound had a tinge of sadness. "But look at me. I'm proof everything Memento Mori has discovered is true. It's all true. And that...that's a scary thought."

"But your notebook said the Wisp can't kill anyone and yet, in the game, she killed Evie hundreds of times," Harold said.

"Whoa, whoa, whoa," I said. "Only one hundred and twelve times."

"I couldn't design a game where the end boss can't kill you," Leda said. "I might not have been the world's greatest video game designer, but I knew I had to change that."

"Why did you add the Wisp's summoning chant to the game if you knew it was real?" I asked.

"I didn't know it was real at the time," Leda said defensively. "If I had known I wouldn't have done it, but I thought it would be fun to add it to the end of the game as a hidden Easter egg. The idea was the player beats the Wisp and wins the game, but then the summoning chant pops up, opening the door for a possible sequel. I swear I had no idea it would actually summon the real Wisp. I wasn't even sure if the Wisp was real before I died."

"About that," Harold said. "Do you remember why the name Morrie was written in your day planner the day you died?"

Leda closed her eyes and nodded. "That was something else I remembered in my office.

Memento Mori found out that I'd hacked their website. I received a letter at work on November first, the day after the game came out. There was no stamp or return address, and no signature—just a drawing of a skull with hourglass eyes, which I'd seen on the website. The letter said they knew what I'd done but also said they were impressed, not mad. They offered to meet with me in a public place—the Victoria Jubilee Fountain in the Halifax Public Gardens—to share even more information in the hopes I'd make a sequel, as long as I promised not to tell anyone anything about Memento Mori—that's why I wrote Morrie in my day planner. I didn't want to ruin my chances—it sounded too good to be true. Unfortunately, as I was crossing the street in front of the Lord Nelson Hotel, everything went black. I didn't even see the car coming."

"And the game," I said. "The glitches. Were those put there on purpose to make it more difficult to beat?"

Leda laughed again, and this time it sounded a little more good-natured. "No. You're familiar with previous efforts from Grim Reapings, *Rainbow Crayon Unicorn* and *Sharkey Shark and the Monkey Munch*. As bad as *Kill Screen* is, it was actually a giant step up from those two games. The glitches in *Kill Screen* turned out to be the key to the game's success, but they were not intentional." She looked at me and smiled. "If you weren't so good at video games, maybe none of this..." She trailed off, and her smile faded fast.

A sick feeling stabbed me in the gut.

"It's not your fault, Evie," she said. "After I died and discovered the Wisp is real, I knew there was a reason no one should beat *Kill Screen*, but I couldn't for the life of me remember what that reason could be. Then I learned that you were close to beating it, and I panicked. I tried to warn you, but I wasn't in my right mind. You didn't know what would happen."

"Thanks," I mumbled.

"So that's why you left?" Harold said. "Because you remembered adding the chant to the game?"

"Yes, but..." Leda hesitated. "I left not only because I remembered what I'd done, but because I remembered what we're up against. And I didn't want you two to be put in harm's way because of a mistake I made. I was hoping you wouldn't come here. We might not all survive."

"We have to try," I said, feeling a little courage return.

"It's not going to be easy," Leda said.

"Maybe not, but I have an idea how to beat the Wisp," I said.

"But to get to her, you have to get through them." Leda pointed past Old Town Clock, up the hill.

The fog had dissipated a little. I could now see Fort George's closest wall. Standing on top of it, staring down at us, were three nasty-looking ghosts.

CHAPTER 18

THEY SLOWLY FADED OUT OF sight. "Who are they?"
I asked Leda.

"I don't know," she said. "But they didn't look
happy to see us."

I nodded. The way they had looked at us
reminded me of the ghosts that had to be beaten
in *Kill Screen* in order to get to the Wisp. One
was a young woman in an old-fashioned gray
dress, another was a man in a red military uniform, and the third, standing apart from the

two adults, was a girl with long, wavy red hair who looked about eight years old. I didn't know why, but the girl creeped me out the most. She looked more like an antique porcelain doll than a kid.

"You might not know them, but I do," Harold said.

"What?"

"I know them," he repeated. "You don't remember?"

I shook my head.

Harold sighed, as if he wasn't surprised. "Guess you weren't paying much attention during our field trip. The tour guide told us a few ghost stories when we were in the museum—the Cavalier Building, I think it was called. He said there have been hundreds of ghost sightings over the years, but the three that are most often seen are known as the Gray Lady, the Sergeant, and the Cuckoo Girl. Now do you remember?"

"It still doesn't ring a bell," I said with a

shrug. "Wait! Didn't the Cavalier Building also have a café?"

"Yeah, I think so. On the main floor."

"They had really good french fries."

"Of course you remember that," Harold said.

"The Wisp must've chosen this location because those three ghosts are already here," Leda said. "With their help, she'll be able to use the Citadel as a portal from the Netherrealm into this world and summon even more ghosts."

"Well, then," I said, tightening my grip on the plastic bag full of salt, "what are we waiting for?"

Harold and I paid the youth rate to get in. I almost asked to buy an adult ticket for Leda.

"What's in the bags?" the teenage ticket seller said from inside his booth.

"Oh, these? Salt, nothing but salt," I said,

trying to sound like it wasn't weird at all that Harold and I were carrying bags of salt. "We had to do some grocery shopping before coming here. You know, for our parents."

"Yup," Harold added. "They wanted salt, and it couldn't wait."

I cringed and then widened my smile, hoping I looked trustworthy and pleasant but fearing I might not. Harold was not cut out for lying, not even white lies.

"That's a lot of salt," the ticket guy said. His eyes were half-closed and he looked like he might fall asleep at any moment. "Place is pretty much empty, probably 'cause of the fog, so at least you won't have to worry about bumping into anyone with your...salt. Anyway, enjoy your visit." He waved us through.

We walked far enough away from the ticket booth so that we wouldn't be overheard. Like the ticket guy had said, the place was empty. No tourists, no ghosts, and no visible Wisp.

"So," I said, "where do you think those three ghosts might be?"

He shrugged. "No idea. They could be anywhere."

"Should we split up?" Leda asked. "There are three of us and three of them. We might find them faster that way."

I shook my head. "I think it would be safer to stick together. We don't really know what we're up against." And the thought of creeping around alone in a fog-filled haunted fort was not appealing, but I kept that to myself.

"Why don't we start by looking in the Cavalier Building?" Harold suggested.

It was as good a place as any. The building—a large, rectangular, three-story structure—emerged through the fog as we crossed the courtyard. We stepped inside the café, and my mouth watered as the smell of fresh-baked cookies wafted under my nose. All the lights were on, but the room had a bleak feeling, thanks to the fog pressing up against the windows. There was an elderly woman working behind the counter and four adults sipping hot drinks at a table beside a large old map of the fort, but otherwise the café was empty. The fog really had kept most people away, which was a lucky break.

"Can I get you dearies anything?" the woman behind the counter asked with a British accent. Her name tag read MAGGIE.

"No," I said, wishing I had time for a quick bite, "we're okay. But I don't suppose..." I trailed off, wondering how to ask my strange question.

Before I finished the thought, Maggie said, "Ghosts, love. I believe you've come to see the ghosts."

I was stunned. "How did you know?"

"Every other day we get a group come in asking the same thing. Let me guess: Jeremy Sinclair?"

"Huh?" I asked, wishing I could've thought of something more intelligent to say.

"He's an author, love. If it wasn't one of his

books, I suppose you read about the Citadel being haunted online and decided to come see for yourself."

I nodded quickly. "Yes, that's right."

"Well, if you're looking for the Gray Lady, she's usually spotted upstairs, in the Army Museum. It's self-guided, so you'll have the place to yourselves. I don't put much stock in ghosts myself—never have seen one—but you two kids have a good time searching for Slimer." She flashed an incredibly warm smile that brightened the room.

Two of the adults at the table chuckled. They'd stopped talking and were listening to us. If they knew the truth they wouldn't be laughing, but I wasn't about to fill them in. That would get us a one-way ticket out of the fort.

I thanked Maggie—she smiled again—and followed Harold up the stairs to the second floor. Leda stayed close behind me.

"I don't know what's so funny about ghosts," she said, sounding a little hurt.

"Don't take it personally," I said. "Maybe they're better off not knowing the truth. My mother always used to say 'Ignorance is bliss.'"

"*Used* to?" Leda asked.

I'd forgotten she didn't know. "My parents died two years ago. Car crash."

"I'm sorry to hear that."

"Hey," I said on a whim. "If you ever meet a Scott and Shannon Vanstone from Wolfville..." I trailed off as I realized how ridiculous what I'd been asking was. Did I really think Leda might accidentally bump into my parents?

Leda understood what I'd left unsaid. "If I ever meet them, I'll tell them they have an incredible daughter who loves them very much." She smiled warmly.

I knew she was humoring me a little, but I didn't mind. Her kindness made me feel good, and I smiled back.

Harold opened a door, and we walked into the museum. It was one long room with hardwood floors and a rounded, white ceiling. Military relics and replicas—medals, war souvenirs, a model of the Vimy Ridge Memorial, a giant cone-shaped bugler's megaphone—filled the space.

I flinched. A man stared us down from within a glass display cabinet. He wore a military uniform, and his eyes were creepy and vacant. I thought for a second or two that it was a ghost, but it turned out to be a mannequin.

"He freaked me out," I said.

"Oh, don't be afraid of him," a voice as smooth as silk said from the far end of the room.

It was the Gray Lady. "Be afraid of me."

CHAPTER 19

SHE LOOKED LIKE A SHADOW come to life, only she wasn't alive.

"Can you see her?" I whispered to Harold.

"Yeah, I can see her," he whispered back.

Her dress was made of faded gray fabric. It was old-fashioned with a high collar, ruffled sleeves, and lace at the neckline and hem. But it wasn't the only thing gray about her. Her complexion was ashen, the same color as an overcast sky, and only a little lighter than her clothes.

Her face was bony, like a skull stripped of flesh wrapped in a thin layer of flayed skin. Pinned on top of her head was a nest of dark hair, black as coal.

I didn't dare reach for the salt. I was afraid that the Gray Lady would lash out the moment I did.

Maybe I could buy us some time by talking while we waited for an opening to strike.

"We're not afraid of you," I said in a deep voice. It would've been great to have a Ghost Box piercing, like in *Kill Screen*, but (a) my grandmother would have never let me pierce my tongue, not in a million years, and (b) this wasn't a video game and Ghost Boxes didn't exist. "And you shouldn't be afraid of us. We are not your enemy."

If the sound of my voice had any effect on her, she didn't show it. She drifted around the room as I spoke, keeping her distance and her eyes away from me. Then she stopped moving and stared at me intently.

"Really? We're not enemies? Then tell me, why are you here?"

"We're here to stop a spirit called the Wisp," I said. There was no point lying—I had a feeling she already knew the truth.

"Heavens no, that simply won't do," she said.

"Have you met her?" Harold said. "Is she here?"

"Yes, I've met her, and yes, she's here," the Gray Lady said, confirming what I suspected.

"Where is she?" I demanded.

"I'll never tell," she whispered in a singsong voice.

"She means to release every evil ghost from the Netherrealm to kill the living," Leda said impatiently.

"And why should you, as a fellow ghost, be opposed to that?" the Gray Lady said, replacing her sweet tone with a hint of venom.

"Once she has killed everyone, she'll be in complete control. She'll reap every last soul and do who-knows-what to us. How can you not be opposed to that?"

"Simple." The Gray Lady straightened her dress and checked her reflection in the glass of a display case. She pulled her lips back and examined her teeth, running her tongue over each one, then blew herself a kiss and, satisfied with her appearance, turned back to us. "My groom died in this building, so I chose to join him, to be together again...for all eternity. But he was gone. If I help the Wisp, she promised to reunite us. We can be together forever."

The Wisp can do that? I wondered in awe.

The Gray Lady clasped her hands together and started to approach us slowly. She stepped one foot forward, paused briefly, stepped her other foot forward, and then repeated her formal pace.

"He died a long time ago," she continued. "November 17, 1900, to be exact. But it feels like yesterday. It was our wedding day."

She continued to walk in an odd, jarring

fashion. At first I thought it was some sort of military march, but then it dawned on me. She was walking as if the museum was a church aisle, and she was approaching her groom.

Her voice was once again soft and sweet, but I didn't trust her tone at all. It made my skin crawl. "I was beginning to lose hope, but then the Wisp arrived today and told me she could find him and bring him back to me. She's preparing for the summoning now. And I can't let you interfere."

The Gray Lady suddenly sped up, faster than I'd ever seen anyone move—living or dead. It was as if she could pass through space or time. She wrapped one of her arms around Leda's neck and dragged her out of our reach.

She yelled when she spoke next, so loud and powerful that I could feel vibrations in the air, and my eardrums pulsed with every word. "The Wisp warned me about ghosts like you! She said there'd be those who try to stop us from completing our task. But I'm not concerned, because she also told me something else."

Leda groaned as the Gray Lady yanked her head backward and put her mouth beside Leda's ear. The Gray Lady spoke in a stage whisper, watching Harold and me as she did. She wanted us to hear her.

"The Wisp told me how to kill another ghost. I didn't think that was possible. How can you kill something that's already dead? But I'm curious." She smiled at us and her teeth gleamed, bright white points amid her grayness. "Let's find out if it works, shall we?"

CHAPTER 20

I STEPPED FORWARD, READY TO tackle the Gray Lady
if I needed to.

"Stay back!" she shouted. "Or I'll make this as
painful for her as possible."

I froze.

"Good girl. And don't even think about reaching into that bag of yours. You too, boy." She cast
a glance at Harold. "Don't think I haven't seen
the way you've both been looking down at them.
You must have something you think is pretty
powerful. Let me guess. Salt?"

I shrugged and nodded. I didn't see any reason to lie.

"Drop them," the Gray Lady said.

Harold and I both hesitated for a moment, but then I sighed and dropped my bag to the floor. Harold did the same.

"Good." She moved her gaze from us to Leda.

"Now it's time for you to die a second death." She closed her eyes, placed her free hand on top of Leda's head, and began to chant in the same language that had summoned the Wisp after I'd beat *Kill Screen*.

I scanned the museum, hoping to find a miracle. My eyes landed on a megaphone, the same one I'd spotted when we first walked into the museum. It was huge, as long as a bike and with a mouth as wide as a hula hoop.

It wasn't a Ghost Box, but it was worth a shot. I bent under the red rope, stepped behind the megaphone, put both hands on its sides to brace myself, and pressed my lips right up against the mouthpiece. And then I yelled.

"RELEASE HER THIS INSTANT!"

My entire body tensed as the sound reverberated through it. My ears rang painfully, and I groaned as I stumbled back from the megaphone. My voice continued to echo throughout the small room.

It worked. The Gray Lady shrieked, and her skin rippled and shimmered from the sound waves. She released Leda and staggered backward without taking her eyes off me. My voice had the same impact on Leda, but at least she was free.

I had no idea how long we had before the effect wore off, so I grabbed a box of salt, took a few quick strides forward, and shook some of the salt in the Gray Lady's face while she was distracted. She shrieked and retreated further, her gray skin sizzling and smoking where she'd been hit by the salt, but she still didn't disappear entirely. My mind raced, but I couldn't think what else to do.

Fortunately, Harold didn't waste any time. Faster than I'd ever seen him move, he grabbed a large metal wrench from a display and ran to my side. He swung it two-handed, like a baseball bat. It passed straight through the Gray Lady's face; her head dissolving into tiny glittering specks of dust. Her scream continued to be heard even though she no longer had a mouth to scream out of, and the rest of her body fell apart and followed her head dust—first up into the air, then in a loop, and finally straight down through the floor where she'd stood.

Suddenly the museum sounded unnaturally quiet.

I laughed and leapt at Harold, giving him a tight hug. "You did it!"

Harold's eyes were wide and his mouth hung open in shock. "Did I?"

"Yes! Well, I stunned her, but you smacked her with the wrench and sent her...wherever she went."

"Yeah, I guess I did," Harold said as his bewildered look was slowly replaced with a proud smile. He tossed the wrench end over end in the air and caught it. It nearly clipped Leda's nose.

"Whoa!" she yelled as she raised her hands in front of her face and stepped back.

Harold grimaced. "Sorry-sorry-sorry!" he said, the three words fused together into one. Then, just for good measure, he added, "Sorry."

"It's all right," Leda said. "Just watch where you point that thing, okay?"

"Of course, of course."

Once they'd both calmed down, our attention fell to the spot where the Gray Lady had disappeared through the floor.

"Is she...?" Harold asked.

"Um, dead?" I said. "I don't know. I don't think so, but I have a feeling that if she's not gone for good, she won't be back anytime soon."

"Let's hope you're right," Leda said.

"Why did this even work?" Harold asked, looking at the wrench in his hands.

There was a small sign on the display shelf where Harold had grabbed the wrench. I pointed at the sign and said, "That's a tank wrench. Says here it's made of iron." I smiled. "And just like salt, iron is one of the types of ammunition the soul-burner fires in *Kill Screen*!"

"You weren't kidding when you told us you did a lot of research," Harold told Leda.

Leda nodded, but her eyes had a faraway look. "I wish we had my notebook. It might help us figure out what to do next."

I smiled and pulled the notebook out of my pocket.

"Flip to the end!" Leda said excitedly. "I think the last thing I wrote about was how the Wisp can summon other ghosts."

I turned to the final page, quickly scanned it, and read the second-to-last paragraph aloud.

Summoning

Great deal of energy needed (even for an entity as powerful as the Wisp!).

Steps:

- Summoning spirit needs to be hidden to avoid interruptions.

- Needs to be near a spirit portal, someplace a ghost can already pass through.

- Then will put their mind into higher state of thought and cognition (like meditation). Might take two or three hours, maybe more.

- Summoning words need to be recited to "open the gate" (for lack of a better term).

- Finally, a noise loud enough to be heard down in the depths

of the Netherrealm needs to be
created, signaling to all that it
is time to rise.

And then I read the final paragraph.

If this is allowed to happen...game
over.

CHAPTER 21

GAME OVER. THE FINAL TWO words in Leda's note-book switched on the gamer in me. My heart beat a little faster and my fingers twitched, pressing invisible buttons. I had to beat the Wisp.

It was only a game.

A game in which the villains were ghosts, and they were very, very real. A game that I couldn't lose or everyone in the world would die.

Yeah, only a game.

I took a deep breath and looked at Harold. His

face was pale, his forehead was beaded in sweat, and his eyes were shut tight.

"Harold?" I said. He didn't respond. "Harold!"

His eyes flew open and took a moment to focus.

"Together, the three of us can beat the Wisp," I said. "But I need you to stay calm, Harold. We all need to be on our A game."

"I know," Harold said with a nod. "I'm fine."

"You know more about this fort than Evie and me," Leda told Harold. "Do you have any idea where the Wisp might be hiding? Take your time."

But not too *much time*, I thought. "Anything will help. Anything at all."

"Well," Harold said, pausing for a moment. "Your notes said she needs to be near a spirit portal—which is, what? A spot where someone died and became a ghost?"

"Could be," Leda said.

"The Gray Lady jumped off this roof, and the

woman in the café said she's often seen here, so her portal is likely here, too. Maybe the Wisp is somewhere in this building."

"Perfect," I said, genuinely relieved. "Let's search the rest of the building."

Harold and I picked up our bags of salt, and the three of us walked toward the door. I stopped suddenly.

"What is it?" Harold asked, his voice a few octaves higher than usual. "V? Do you see another ghost?" He tightened his grip on the wrench.

I shook my head and picked up what I'd seen that had stopped me in my tracks. "A shovel?" Harold said.

I nodded. "An *iron* shovel."

❦

We walked through the entire building, all three floors, but found nothing unusual. There were a few off-limits rooms we couldn't open, but after listening at the doors for a few minutes, none of us could hear a sound from the other side. With every passing minute, I grew more and more determined to find the Wisp and stop her before she could summon a single ghost, but I was also growing frustrated.

Think, V. If you were a wisp, where would you go?

"We saw three ghosts as we approached," I said. "There are probably two other portals."

Leda nodded. "The Wisp could be hiding near one of the other two."

"So where'd they die?" I asked. "Do you remember anything, Harold?"

He shrugged with a frown. "The guide said something about the Sergeant falling down a well, but I have no idea where that could be."

I had one of those moments where it felt like a lightbulb had been switched on above my head. "I know someone who might know."

I led Harold and Leda back to the café; Harold

agreed to take the wrench and shovel and meet me outside in a few minutes. I didn't think the woman who worked there would be too impressed that we'd borrowed them from the museum, even if I told her they'd saved our lives. Inside, the patrons who had been there before were gone, and Maggie was putting the chairs up on the tables.

"We're open, dearie," she said, her voice still sweet as honey. "Just thought I'd get a jump on my closing duties since it's so quiet today. Did you have any luck finding your ghost?"

"No," I lied. "But that's kind of why I came here. My friend and I heard that maybe there's another ghost lingering around the well." I'd gone out on a limb and made that up, of course, but I figured it was worth a shot.

She shook her head. "Sorry, love. I've worked here for more than twenty years, and I've never seen a well."

But how could that be? I wanted to scream. *Harold was told the Sergeant...*

My eyes settled on the large old-fashioned map on the wall where the customers had sat before.

I noticed a small circle across the courtyard from the Cavalier Building. The circle was south of the front gate and the noon gun. Beneath the circle, written in calligraphy, was the word *Well*.

"Well, I'll be," Maggie said, then chuckled at her own joke. "I've never noticed that before. They must've taken out the well and covered the hole years ago."

"Thanks for all your help," I said over my shoulder as I raced out the door.

I met back up with Harold and Leda, and we searched the grounds near the front gate, hoping to find the Wisp before the Sergeant showed up. We raced around most of the courtyard, widening our search, but still didn't find anything. After a few minutes, we circled back to the front gate. Just then, a man materialized out of the fog. My body tensed before I realized it was one of the patrons from the café. He was followed by the other three. They gave Harold and me odd looks—I guessed that was probably because of the shovel and large wrench we now held—as they passed and then were swallowed up by the fog as they exited the fort.

"Either the Sergeant isn't here," I said once we were alone, "or we're in the wrong place."

"Could the map have been wrong?" Leda asked.

"I doubt it," Harold said. "It was a military map and—"

I held up my hand and said, "Wait. What's that?" I thought I had seen some movement, some shadow through the fog—something dark and wide. I couldn't tell what I thought I'd seen, or if I'd actually seen anything at all. The fog acted like a blanket that cut out all background noise—traffic, birds, wind. It was like we were in a cocoon without any of the safety of the chrysalis, and I suddenly felt very exposed.

"V?" Harold whispered.

I continued to stare ahead.

"V?" Harold whispered again, a little louder and a lot more panicked.

I took a step forward.

The shadow slowly revealed itself.

It was a well—an old, stone water well covered in moss that had definitely not been there a moment ago.

"What the...?" Leda said.

A hand slipped over the top row of rock, gripped the lip of the well, and pulled up a water-logged body.

CHAPTER 22

I'D GROWN MOSTLY ACCUSTOMED TO the sight of ghosts during the past two years. Mostly. But when I watched the Sergeant crawl out of the phantom well and land on the ground of the parade square, all thought left my head.

He was dressed in a military uniform with a three-bar chevron on each sleeve. His head sported a beret, and his boots were black. His clothes were drenched and dripping with water, but his body... His body simultaneously repulsed and fascinated me. I couldn't look away.

His face was bloated and bluish in color. His swollen stomach stretched his shirt to its breaking point—I supposed his internal organs had soaked up as much water as they could. And the skin of his hands and face was covered in wrinkles. I imagined that his entire body, head to foot, looked like a giant, pale blue raisin. The thought made me want to throw up.

"You cannot stop the Wisp. We will make sure of that," the Sergeant said. Brackish, bloody water bubbled out of his mouth and dribbled down his chin as he spoke.

"That's disgusting," Harold said.

I steadied my nerves and raised my chin, wishing I had a giant megaphone with me. "By 'we' do you mean you and the other two ghosts in the fort?"

The Sergeant nodded.

"I've got news for you," I said, feeling a

little like an actor playing a part on a TV show like *Screamers*. "We've already beaten the Gray Lady."

A brief look of shock passed over the Sergeant's face. "No matter. There's still me...and the girl."

I gripped the shovel a little tighter and stood up straighter. "We're not afraid of you," I said, trying my best to sound convincing.

A crooked smile spread slowly across the Sergeant's face. "You should be afraid. If not of me, then definitely of her."

I laughed once. "She's what? Eight years old? I'm pretty sure we can handle her."

The Sergeant didn't respond. His sick smile stretched wider. I realized that his gaze had shifted from me to something to my left.

Harold and Leda turned around and looked at whatever held the Sergeant's full attention.

I didn't turn to look. I had a feeling, and it wasn't good.

"She's right behind me, isn't she?" I said.

"Tick-tock." It was a young, high-pitched voice at my back. She sounded close. Too close.

I turned around slowly. It felt like I was moving underwater, like I was fighting a gentle resistance in the air.

Standing a few feet away was the Cuckoo Girl. She had round cheeks and dark eyes, and the top of her head came up to my chin. Her dress was black, her skin glowed faintly, and her hair was white—but it didn't look like it had always been that shade. She didn't look angry or intimidating or vengeful. She looked sad.

Just then the Cuckoo Girl's face flickered, as if she had two faces—one visible, one hidden. The eyes on this second face, which I'd only seen for a heartbeat or two, burned with anger; her lips pulled back, revealing her teeth like those of a wolf on the prowl.

For a moment I felt like giving up. I considered tossing my shovel and salt to the ground, raising my hands in the air, and slowly walking away.

But how much time would that buy me? Enough to find Grandma and tell her I loved her one last time before the Wisp emptied the Netherrealm and her spirits killed us all?

And besides, I was far too competitive to admit defeat or to give up. I looked at Harold and Leda; they didn't look like warriors, but we'd made it this far, and we had beat the Gray Lady together. If either was considering giving up, their stony faces didn't show it.

We could do this. We *would* do this.

"You two take the Sergeant," I said to Harold and Leda. I didn't bother trying to conceal my words. We were past that. "I'll take her."

"I have all the time in the world," the Cuckoo Girl said in a sweetly innocent tone. "But your time is about to end."

I charged.

CHAPTER 23

I SWUNG THE SHOVEL. THE Cuckoo Girl ducked it easily, using her size to her advantage. I had hoped that by charging her so suddenly she'd be caught off guard, and I could end the fight before it had begun, but no such luck.

"Nice try," she said, "but you'll have to do better than that."

That was my plan. I swung again the moment she finished speaking, but she flew backward out of my reach. She was clearly scared of the shovel and hadn't taken her eyes off it since I'd first charged her.

"I was there, you know," she said. "I saw what happened to the Gray Lady when your friend, that boy, hit her with the wrench."

She pointed at Harold when she said "that boy." He and Leda were doing a good job keeping the Sergeant on his toes, circling him on opposite sides so that he couldn't attack them at the same time.

Don't get too close, Harold, I thought. *Be careful.*

"You were in the museum," I said, turning my attention back to the Cuckoo Girl, "and you didn't do anything to stop us from hurting the Gray Lady?"

"I don't care about her," she said with a sneer.

"Then why are you helping the Wisp?"

"Simple: I want to watch the world burn."

"Why?"

"Because the world did nothing to save me."

Her face fell again, only this time I suspected her sadness wasn't a mask. "One minute I'm here with my parents, the next I'm dead, and I have no idea how. All I know is no one protected me—not my parents, not the soldiers—no one! Everyone moved on. I was left behind. So I watch. And I follow. Sometimes I grab people's hands. Sometimes my touch hurts them. Sometimes..." Her eyes were glassy and unfocused. "Sometimes my touch kills them."

I tried not to imagine all the people who the Cuckoo Girl had killed over the years, people who had likely been suspected of dying from other causes, like a heart attack or a stroke.

"You don't have to do this," I said. Maybe I could get her to change her mind. Maybe it wasn't too late. But those were a couple of big maybes. "What the Wisp wants...is good for no one. Not you or me or my friends. Once we're all ghosts, she's going to use us however she wants."

The Cuckoo Girl cocked her head to the side and considered this for a moment. I started to think my words had actually gotten through to her, but then she shrugged.

"I don't care," she said.

Out of the corner of my eye I saw Harold throw his wrench at the Sergeant. It sailed wide and missed the ghost by a few inches.

I felt doubt roll into my mind like a thundercloud. It made me wonder if this was a game I couldn't win. No, it was worse than wondering. The feeling was closer to *knowing*.

I knew I wouldn't be able to save myself. I knew I wouldn't be able to save my friends. I knew I wouldn't be able to save anyone, just like I couldn't save my parents.

"Enough," I said, startling myself a little with the sound of my voice. I hadn't meant to speak out loud.

"What?" the Cuckoo Girl asked. She paced left and right, keeping her eyes on the shovel, looking, I knew, for a weakness, some way she could attack me.

"I said 'enough.' Your parents are gone."

The Cuckoo Girl gave me a curious look, her eyes narrowed. There was anger in her stare. I didn't know my parents appearing the night before they died was anything but a dream, so how could I have helped them? I couldn't have. But this time, if I allowed doubt to convince me that I couldn't save myself, my friends, or anyone else, I wouldn't get to walk away—if I got to walk away at all—with a clear conscience. Because I *did* have the chance to help. I *did* have the ability to do something. I just had to let go of my guilt, the same guilt that made me quit sports and spend most of my free time the past two years pressing buttons and "living" in one fictional world after the other.

Enough, I told myself one more time.

I lunged at the Cuckoo Girl, and her eyes went wide. Maybe she finally saw me as a threat, or maybe she just thought I was as determined as she was, but she flew away. Not just a few feet, but all the way to the top of the wall above the front entrance. I turned to see how Harold and Leda were doing. My heart sank. They weren't doing well.

Unarmed, Harold had no defense against the Sergeant. He tried to dodge an attack, but the Sergeant wrapped his arms around Harold's shoulders. Harold yelled out in pain—it sounded like he was being burned alive.

The Cuckoo Girl had said she'd killed people simply by touching them, and from the sounds that were coming out of Harold, it was clear the Sergeant could do the same.

Harold was going to die. They were far away. I raised the shovel and began to run, hoping I would make it in time.

But I didn't need to.

Leda looked from the Sergeant to the wrench Harold had thrown. It had landed close to her feet.

The Sergeant dragged Harold backward to the well. Harold yelled and moaned, gut-wrenching sounds that began to dwindle as he lost strength. His arms fell limp at his sides, and he stopped kicking his feet.

Harold was completely at the Sergeant's will. The ghost pulled Harold onto the edge of the well. Leda bent down. She reached out her hand. She paused, but only for a brief second. And then she grabbed the iron wrench and quickly stood back up. She yelled out in pain, and her body began to dissolve almost immediately.

"No!" I yelled, willing my legs to run faster.

Leda threw the wrench with the last of her strength. It flew through the air, end over end, with a *whoosh-whoosh-whoosh* sound and struck the Sergeant's forehead as he pulled Harold down into the well.

Both Leda and the Sergeant turned into the same smokelike light as the Gray Lady, and their dust swirled in the air for a moment before streaming down into the earth. The Sergeant's well did the same, and Harold fell through the air a short distance and landed on the ground. He lay on his back, unmoving.

I stopped running with a halt. Not because I didn't know if my friend was dead or alive. Not because the ghost who had helped us make it this far had sacrificed herself to save Harold. Because an explosion had filled the air above my head. It was so loud that I thought the Wisp had blown up the world, but then I remembered something Leda had written in her notebook:

Finally, a noise loud enough to be heard down in the depths of the Netherrealm needs to be created, signaling to all that it is time to rise.

I looked up and saw the Cuckoo Girl. She was standing atop the Citadel's wall, beside a smoking cannon. The noon gun.

She was smiling like a kid on Christmas morning.

The ground trembled slightly. The tremble turned into a shake. The shake became a quake. A terrible sound of rocks splitting and grinding and tumbling filled the air.

I spun around just in time to see the center of the Citadel's courtyard split in half. A haze of foggy blue light filtered out of the earth and lit the fort.

And then the first ghost crawled out of the jagged hole, followed by a second, a third, a fourth, a fifth... Soon there were ten, twenty, fifty...

Hundreds.

CHAPTER 24

THE GHOSTS FILLED THE PARADE square, each one more nightmarish than the last.

Most might have passed for living, except for the telltale blue glow surrounding them and their dead eyes. But then there were the others...

There was a man who more closely resembled a skeleton than a spirit; a woman with no lips and exposed bloodstained teeth; a skinny man nearly seven feet tall with no face—just a thick membrane of skin where his eyes, nose, and mouth should've been. A young girl—not the Cuckoo Girl—whose hair was on fire; a pair of identical twins who crawled across the ground like spiders; a sad clown, his face paint smeared and his colorful outfit torn to shreds; a person—I couldn't tell if it was a man or a woman—whose body inexplicably looked like it had been turned inside out.

And still they kept on coming.

There was nothing we could do. We were trapped.

"Listen, Harold," I said, feeling oddly at peace. "If you want to run, I won't blame you. I'll hold them back as long as I can and give you a head start."

He looked like he might cry or throw up or pass out—maybe one after the other—but he shook his head. "No. I'm staying with you." He picked up the wrench and stood close to my side.

I nodded. "Good. We might not stand a chance, but let's take down as many of these creatures as possible."

Harold returned my nod, but then he frowned.

"Wait," he said, and ran a few feet away.

"Harold? What are you doing?"

The first ghost—Skeleton Man—was closing in fast and would be at my throat in seconds.

Harold grabbed our Pete's Fine Foods bags and raced back to my side. He dropped them, took out a box of salt, opened it, and poured its contents in a circle around us. He closed the circle just as Skeleton Man reached us. The ghost stopped as suddenly as if he'd run face-first into an invisible force field.

"Harold! You're a genius!" I wrapped my arms around him and gave him a tight squeeze.

"Thanks," he said, his voice muffled by my shoulder. "But I got the idea from you. Remember?" The other ghosts were right behind Skeleton Man. First Lipless, followed by Skinny Man, Burning Girl, the Spider Twins, Sad Clown, and Inside-Out Thing. The other ghosts joined them, closing in all around us. They yelled and screamed and moaned, but none of them were able to cross the circle of salt. "The new problem is," Harold said, "we're kinda stuck."

How long would the ghosts wait around the ring? Probably forever. How long until Harold and I starved to death or died of dehydration? Maybe a week or ten days, tops. How long before we lost our minds? My guess was one day. Probably less.

I waved off his concern and made a *pfft* sound with my lips. "Just wait. We'll think of something." That's when I caught a glimpse of the Cuckoo Girl through the motley crew of ghosts. She was still on the Citadel wall, but something south of the fort had caught her attention. It was hard to tell for sure from such a distance, but she looked concerned, or at the very least surprised. She flew off the wall and dropped out of sight.

It wasn't long before I saw what the Cuckoo Girl had seen. Ten seconds after she'd jumped off the wall, another ghost took her place.

It was Tie-Dye, the old man with the gray beard. I couldn't believe it, nor could I figure out how one old ghost had scared off such an intimidating spirit as the Cuckoo Girl.

And then it became clear. Tie-Dye wasn't alone.

He had brought his friends. The ghosts who had stopped me on the street as I'd walked toward the fog-enshrouded Citadel.

And, by the looks of it, about two hundred more ghosts.

They took up places on the wall. And as I turned around in a circle I saw that they had surrounded the Citadel.

"Harold? Can you see what I see?"

He nodded. "It's an army," he said in awe.

I smiled. "An army that's come to make a final stand."

And then the battle began.

CHAPTER 25

WE HAVE A CHANCE, I thought. But we weren't free and clear yet. The two sides were roughly equal in number, but there was no way Tie-Dye's ghosts were as ferocious as the spirits of the Netherrealm.

The worst of the worst—Skeleton Man and his crew—were still surrounding Harold's ring of salt.

They were within striking distance.

"Harold," I whispered. "Let's grab some salt—"

"And even the playing field," he whispered back.

While the ghosts stared at the newcomers on the walls and waited for whatever was about to happen next—the calm before the storm—Harold and I crouched and grabbed two boxes each. We opened them, stood up slowly, and—

"Now!" I shouted.

We flung the salt as quickly and as widely as possible, covering the ghosts closest to us. The effect on them was immediate and totally gross. It hissed and crackled and steamed on contact. The ghosts screamed in pain. The salt burned their bodies, causing their skin to bubble and split and disintegrate. It covered Skeleton Man's forearm, and his skin slid off his bones like a latex glove. A large amount of salt landed on the back of one of the Spider Twins as he skittered in circles. After a while the salt split him clean in half. Lipless's cheeks and forehead were hit first by me from the right and second by Harold from the left, and soon her lips weren't the only part of her face to be missing.

We sprayed the others, too—Skinny Man, Burning Girl, the second Spider Twin, Sad Clown, and Inside-Out Thing. That last ghost was the worst of all. For a moment I had this weird idea that the salt might make Inside-Out Thing turn right side out or something. But it didn't. When the salt hit it... Let's just say it was the most disgusting thing I've ever seen in my life.

Harold laughed, sounding half relieved and half insane. I knew how he felt.

"It worked!" he said. "That was awesome!"

Flinging all that salt around had made me feel a little like a professional athlete who'd just won the World Series and was dousing her coach and teammates in Gatorade. Only, of course, I'd used salt and I'd doused the enemy, not my teammates. But still, I felt pretty good.

"Hopefully that helps them," I said.

Tie-Dye had led the charge while we'd taken out Skeleton Man and the others closest to us, and the good ghosts had swarmed off the walls and were dragging the evil spirits back down to the Netherrealm through the crack in the ground. They were putting up a good fight, too, but I was still worried. I picked up the shovel and then the wrench, which I handed to Harold. He took it, and I noticed his grip was a lot firmer now.

"I don't think we'll be able to sit out the rest of this fight," I said.

"Me neither," he responded. "We need to help them."

I slapped Harold's shoulder, offered him a smile, and stepped out of the salt ring. A Netherrealm ghost floated past, and I swung the shovel through her chest. She howled, dissipated, swirled in the air, and flew down through the ground.

A ghost shrieked in my ear, so close that I could feel a slight icy breeze on the back of my neck. I wouldn't have time to turn and defend myself. I hadn't tricked myself into thinking I'd make it out of this alive, but I hadn't thought I'd be killed so soon.

The ghost shrieked again, and I waited for it to dig into me with its teeth or nails or whatever.

Nothing happened.

A second or two passed, and my shoulders and neck relaxed. I turned slowly.

Harold was smiling at me with a slightly goofy grin. The ghost was gone.

"You owe me one, V," he said.

"Thank you," I said.

We stood back-to-back and continued to swing. I took out three more ghosts. Harold took out four. I didn't know he had it in him. I doubt he knew he had it in him. But my arms were getting tired and, by the look on Harold's face, he was fatigued, too. The Wisp's ghosts were slowly overtaking Tie-Dye's ghosts. I scanned the square but couldn't see Tie-Dye anywhere. I hoped he was okay.

A swarm of ghosts caught on to what Harold

and I were doing and formed a line. There were eight or ten, and instead of blindly rushing toward us, they waited, murmuring something I couldn't quite hear. And then they bent their line into the shape of a horseshoe, curving around us and slowly approaching from three sides.

"I think this is it," I told Harold.

He didn't respond, because the horseshoe gang froze, then turned to look behind them. They heard something. Soon I heard it, too.

A great *whoosh*, as if a dam had broken and a rush of water was racing toward us.

It was coming from the crack in the ground. It wasn't water. It was blue, and bright...

Ghosts. More ghosts. They didn't look quite so...human as Tie-Dye and his group, but they certainly didn't look as twisted as the ghosts that were attacking us.

I'd never been so happy to see dead people in my life.

They swirled and flew through the fort. The

Wisp's ghosts were completely overwhelmed and, in a few short minutes, the last few had been dragged back down to where they came from.

There was a great cheer from the remaining fifty or so ghosts who'd been part of the first attack with Tie-Dye. The crowd parted, and the old man walked toward us.

"Tie-Dye!" I shouted, racing to his side.

He looked at me quizzically, not quite sure what to make of what I'd said.

I pointed at his chest. "Because of your shirt."

He smiled and nodded. "What's your name?"

"Evie," I said. "But my friends call me V."

A lot of ghosts—the ones he'd come with—had disappeared during the fight.

"I'm sorry that you lost so many of your friends," I said.

His smile faltered for a second but then returned, bigger and more genuine than before. He even smiled with his eyes, and the pinpoints of light in his irises danced. "No, Evie, you have no need to apologize to us. We were scared, and you gave us hope. But, more important, we were adrift, and you gave us purpose. If anything, we need to thank *you*."

The ghosts formed a ring around Harold and me and thanked us. Even though I knew we had one last thing to do, I was happy.

The ground shook and began to shift beneath my feet. The crack was sealing itself up.

Tie-Dye looked at the other spirits and stroked his beard in thought. "I think... I think I'm ready to move on."

The others nodded agreement. "Thank you again, V," Tie-Dye said.

"Maybe we'll meet again," I said. "But not too soon."

"If you see a ghost called Leda, tell her Harold and V say thanks," Harold said.

"I will." Tie-Dye followed the others and was the last to slip into the crack, a moment before it resealed itself.

The afternoon was once again quiet. I was exhausted and sore, right down to my bones.

"What now?" Harold asked.

"I think you know."

"The Wisp."

"That's right."

"Where do you think she is?" Harold asked.

I thought back. Something had stuck in my mind. The Cuckoo Girl, when she had stood on the wall near the entrance. She'd seen Tie-Dye and the others and had fled. But thinking about it then, it was obvious she wouldn't leave. She was committed to helping the Wisp. She would have gone to her.

Find the Cuckoo Girl, find the Wisp.

"I know where we have to go," I said. "The Old Town Clock."

"That's it!" Harold said. "Tick-tock," he added grimly.

CHAPTER 26

WE CAME UP WITH A plan as we ran, carrying our bags in one hand (they were now much lighter) and our iron weapons in the other.

I half expected either the Cuckoo Girl or the Wisp to jump out of the fog, but we managed to reach the Old Town Clock without incident. We stopped at the door to catch our breath.

Harold nodded. He was ready.

So was I. I nodded back, then gripped the door handle. "You remember the plan?"

"Yeah, we literally just came up with it," he said with a nod. "I also remember how weak it is."

"Well, we don't have time to come up with anything else."

"That makes me feel so much better," Harold said with an exaggerated eye roll.

"Glad to hear it," I said as I threw open the door. We rushed into the darkness.

Old Town Clock wasn't large, so even though it was denser with fog than the entire fort had been, it didn't take us long to determine that the first floor was empty.

Harold groaned loudly.

"What's wrong?" I whispered. As close as he was, I could barely see him.

"Before we stepped inside I should have said, 'Ready Player One.' And then you could have said, 'Ready Player Two.' That would have been cool."

"Next time we do something like this we can..." I trailed off. I'd spotted something.

"V?" Harold asked. "What is it?"

I pointed up the stairs. Wreathed in fog and staring down at us with a wicked smile was the Cuckoo Girl.

"You came," she said, sounding both surprised and delighted. "I can't believe it. Well, you're almost out of time. Let's have some fun."

"That's exactly what we came for," I said, and without giving her time to respond, both Harold and I charged up the stairs. We raised our weapons and yelled.

The Cuckoo Girl was caught off guard—maybe even a little afraid, judging by the look on her face—and ran away from us. We hoped she'd lead us to the Wisp.

And she did.

Although it hadn't been long since I'd released the Wisp, I'd already forgotten what it felt like to be in her presence—her overpowering yet gentle stature, her odd way of talking, her contradictory essence.

Looking at her floating in the air, surrounded by mist and holding that glowing orb in front of her chest, made my knees go weak and my head feel heavy.

This is it, V, I told myself. *Don't get cold feet now.*

But it was cold, and not because of my nerves. I could see my breath in front of me and the windows were covered in frost.

The Wisp looked at me with the slightest hint of a smile, but her eyes were like ice. They penetrated my skin and observed my soul, poked at my brain, and read my thoughts. "We meet again, Evie Vanstone. But now, unlike last time, you are no longer a friend of the Netherrealm."

"They brought the army of ghosts to the fort," the Cuckoo Girl spat. "They snuffed out the Gray Lady and the Sergeant."

"Is this true?" the Wisp asked as gently as a mother wishing her sleeping baby good night.

I couldn't move, couldn't speak. I couldn't even open my mouth. My tongue felt like it was swollen, and my throat was painfully dry.

The Wisp laughed, a sound without joy. "No need to answer, Evie. I know what you've done, and I know why you're here." Her eyes narrowed. "You've come to kill us."

I still couldn't speak, but Harold picked up my slack. "There's no use denying it," he said, and raised the wrench.

I'd temporarily lost my courage, and Harold had found it. Seeing that broke me out of my frozen state. I raised the shovel, but the Wisp raised her free hand and made a fist, then quickly spread her fingers. The shovel flew out of my hand and smashed through one of the narrow corner windows. Harold's wrench broke through one of the opposite windows, and the bags of salt followed the shovel and wrench out through the shattered glass. I heard everything hit the ground below.

We were defenseless.

"Wait a minute. Your name. Evie Vanstone...
Evie Vanstone...Evie Vanstone," the Wisp said,
rolling my name around her mouth like a morsel
of meat she was savoring. "I know your parents."

CHAPTER 27

"MY PARENTS?" I SAID, NOT quite believing my own ears. That was a game changer.

I was vaguely aware of Harold beside me, whispering. Something about "stick to the," but I couldn't focus on him. If the Wisp knew my parents...

She nodded. "Yes. They died two years and thirty-seven days ago. They've been trapped in the Netherrealm ever since."

"I don't believe you," I said, hating the way

I sounded, high-pitched and panicked. "You're lying."

"I promise you I am not," she said, but there was a glint in her eyes that made me question what she was saying. "They came to the Netherrealm and, like so many before them and so many since, they couldn't leave. But you have no need to worry that they're neglected..." Her orb grew brighter and the room grew darker. "I make sure to torment them daily."

Whether or not it was true, I had heard enough. I gave Harold a slight nod, then uttered the line I'd said so many times playing *Kill Screen*: "I have come to send you back to the Netherrealm. You are an agent of darkness and are not welcome here among the living." I paused, then added, "This is for my parents."

Harold and I both lunged forward, throwing all of our weight into the ghosts. He into the Cuckoo Girl, and me into the Wisp. For this part of the plan to work we needed neither of them to suspect that we'd attack them unarmed, which is why we tricked the Wisp into getting rid of the shovel, wrench, and salt.

It worked. Neither the Wisp nor the Cuckoo Girl put up much of a fight, at least not at first. Harold yelled in pain but managed to push the Cuckoo Girl through the back wall and into one of the clock faces outside. Her body came into contact with the minute and hour hands, which we'd guessed were made of iron. We couldn't see what happened, but we heard it. She screamed—an anguished sound that, after a brief struggle, ended abruptly.

As Harold took care of the Cuckoo Girl, I struggled with the Wisp. I wrapped my arms around her and held on tight. Touching her didn't hurt, so I pushed her toward the side wall, which also had an iron clock on its exterior. But she yanked me to the corner and we fell backward through one of the broken windows, then plummeted. I thought I was dead meat, but she pulled us both up just before we hit the ground.

We flew through the air, wrapped around each other, heading east. First over Carmichael Street, through the Grand Parade, then over George Street, past a large-scale re-creation of Theodore the Tugboat docked on the wharf, and then over the harbor. It had taken only a few seconds to reach the water.

"You thought you could push me into the clock face and I'd disappear? Die?" The Wisp spoke directly into my ear. I cringed. Her voice sounded like a mixture of a snake's hiss and nails on a chalkboard. "Foolish girl. You can't kill me. Once I've disposed of you, I'll return to the Citadel, claim your friend's soul, and begin summoning more Netherrealm ghosts. And no one will be able to stop me."

"You're right, no one would be able to stop you," I said as I dug my hand into my cargo pants pocket. I looked down. We were high above the harbor and moving fast. I steeled my nerve. "Which is why I need to stop you now!"

I pulled free the box of salt I'd had in my pocket ever since Pete's Fine Foods and sprayed it onto the Wisp's face and neck.

"Waste not, want not," I said, thinking of Grandma and her collection of fast-food salt-and-pepper packs.

The Wisp howled and shrieked as the salt bit into her flesh, opening an angry cut just below her left eye that ran down to the top of her collarbone. She didn't disappear, like the Netherrealm ghosts, but she did use her hands—both of them—to cover her face.

The orb was suspended in midair between us. I grabbed the orb—it was surprisingly cool— and held it tight to my chest, like a wide receiver afraid of dropping a football when the end zone is only ten yards away. As soon as I did, I started to fall. The Wisp continued to soar away, but only for a beat before she realized what had happened.

She stopped moving and looked down at me in outrage, and then she screamed louder than she had when the salt had hit her face—louder than I thought possible—and raced toward me like a rocket.

But I had already fallen far, too far for her to catch. My back broke the surface of the water with a mighty splash. I nearly released the orb but managed to hold on to it as I held my breath and sank deeper.

The Wisp dove through the surface above and glided toward me. The fog that always trailed her continued to swirl around her body.

She spoke a few words in Saancticae and reached desperately for her orb. Her fingers nearly touched its glassy surface...

But then a shadow passed *within* it.

"No!" the Wisp said, and she sounded scared. Not scared and disinterested, or scared and at ease, or any other odd, contradictory combination. Just straight-up scared.

And I knew then that all of this—the plan to have the Wisp disarm us, fly me out over the harbor, to shock her with the salt and make her drop me into the water, all so that the orb would be submerged and the Wisp would be sent back to the Netherrealm—it was all going to work.

"Give me that," the Wisp said, pleading. "Without it, I—"

A small crack appeared on the surface of the orb with a *ping*, then started to spread.

I needed air, but I couldn't surface just yet. I had to see this through, even if it killed me.

I thought of the Gray Lady, the Sergeant, and the Cuckoo Girl. I thought of the Netherrealm ghosts. I thought of Tie-Dye and his followers. I thought of my grandmother. I thought of Harold. I thought of Leda. I thought of the Wisp. But most of all, I thought of my parents.

If I could have spoken, I would have told the Wisp, "You lied about my parents, you—" followed by a not-so-nice name that my parents wouldn't have approved of. But given the circumstances, I think it would have been justified.

As if she had read my mind, the Wisp said, "Your parents passed through the Netherrealm after they died. They didn't stay. I lied. Give me that back before it's destroyed, and I'll find them—I can bring them back to life." She sounded desperate and unnerved, but more than anything she still sounded straight-up scared.

I'd be lying, too, if I said I didn't consider her offer. I never dreamed it would be possible to have my parents back.

In fact, it was an offer I couldn't refuse. If I actually believed her, that is.

Ping! Another crack appeared on the orb's surface, and I pulled it as far out of the Wisp's reach as possible.

She made one final lunge for the orb, but it shattered into a thousand disintegrating pieces, and the murky harbor water was illuminated by the brightest light imaginable.

When the light faded, a man floated between me and the Wisp. He was a small man with a bony face and long, stringy red hair. Like the Wisp, the water didn't appear to have any effect on him.

"I'm free!" he yelled with a mad laugh.

My vision started to fade, I could feel my heartbeat pounding in my ears, and my lungs burned. I needed air. I swam up but looked back down just before reaching the surface, where I saw an awesome sight.

Without the orb to give her power, the Wisp's face split in half. It started at the salt scar and quickly spread right down to her feet. Her body ripped itself apart, and the pieces swirled deep down into the bottom of the harbor, out of sight.

One small ball of light, like a flame or a jewel, remained of the shattered orb. The man—whoever he was—plucked it out of the water and slipped it into his pocket. He looked up at me and said, "Thank you." Then he flew straight past me and into the sky.

I followed him to the water's surface and

sucked in a lungful of air as I treaded in place, but he was gone.

The afternoon was quiet and calm. The fog had lifted.

I waited until I'd caught my breath, then swam to shore.

Air had never tasted sweeter.

CHAPTER 28

"YOUR LIPS ARE BLUE," HAROLD said. He'd arrived just as I was pulling myself out of the water.

I was shaking so hard my teeth were chattering, and water was pooling on the wharf around my feet. I felt like I might never warm up but I didn't care.

We'd done it. We'd actually beat the Wisp—and, if that wasn't enough, an army of evil spirits, too. It sounded nuts, but we'd actually saved the world. If I could do all that, maybe it was time to take Coach up on his offer to rejoin the soccer team. What else was I going to do? Sit around waiting for *Kill Screen 2* to be released?

I laughed weakly, and Harold narrowed his eyes and stared at me like I'd finally lost it. Maybe I had. He took his jacket off and told me to do the same. Normally I'd wave off such an offer but not that day. I handed him my waterlogged jacket and slipped my arms into his warm, dry coat. As my upper body started to warm up, I realized how cold I really was. I'd been numb to it before, but now my bones ached, my skin burned, and my blood felt like ice water.

"C-c-cold," I said. It was all I could manage.

But I could still feel a smile pulling the corners of my mouth upward.

"Let's get you some dry clothes," Harold said. As we walked three blocks south to the Maritime Mall, I filled him in on what he'd missed.

"Do you think the Wisp is actually dead?" Harold asked. "Like, *dead* dead?"

My teeth chattered as I said, "D-d-don't know. I hope so."

"I don't think I ever truly believed we could do it," Harold said. "But we did it. We won." He sounded shocked.

"Th-thanks t-to you," I said, trying not to bite my tongue in half as I spoke.

"Thanks to *you*," Harold said with a smile that faded as he added, "and Leda." He was silent and solemn for a moment, then said, "Not much farther."

I felt better inside the mall, and Harold told me to wait in the women's bathroom as he went to buy me some clothing from a thrift shop. I checked my phone while I waited, but it was toast. Harold returned a few minutes later and knocked, then handed the clothes through the door as I cracked it open. I went into a stall and examined the clothes.

He'd bought me a pair of baggy purple sweatpants, a blue sweater with HALIFAX INTERNATIONAL

TUNA TOURNAMENT SOCIETY printed on it, and a plain white T-shirt that was three sizes too big for me. But I couldn't have cared less, because he also got me a pair of new socks; there's no better feeling than putting on dry socks after you've spent some time treading water in Halifax Harbor in the middle of May.

I was about to leave the bathroom when I heard someone whisper my name.

"Who's there?" I spun around but I was still alone. "Who said that?"

After a tense moment, the voice finally responded. "It's me, Evie. It's Leda."

I opened the stall door. The bathroom was empty.

"Leda?" I asked. "Why can't I see you?"

Silence followed, but I had a feeling I knew why I couldn't see her. I'd lost the ability to see ghosts. Easy come, easy go.

"I can't stay long, Evie," Leda said, "but I just wanted to tell you that I won't stop looking for your parents. And when I find them, I'll tell them what I promised you I would: they have an incredible daughter who loves them very much."

"Thank you, Leda," I said, fighting back tears. "Thanks for everything."

"Thank you, Evie, for helping me right the wrong I created when I added that summoning chant to *Kill Screen*."

There was a gentle touch on my cheek, as if five thin threads of wind had cupped the side of my face, and then I felt a cool breeze rush past. I was alone once more.

I felt human again when I left the bathroom, although I must've looked like an alien from another planet.

Harold took one look at my clothes and groaned. "Sorry, V... I was in a rush."

I gave him a hug and said, "It's perfect."

He looked at me skeptically. "You sure?"

"Well, maybe not perfect, but close enough."

He laughed, and we started to walk back through the mall the way we'd entered.

I didn't know the best way to bring up what had happened in the bathroom, so I blurted it out: "I don't think I can see ghosts anymore, but Leda is okay." Tears welled in my eyes and I quickly wiped them away. "I'll, um, tell you about it later."

Harold thought about what I'd said for a moment and then nodded and said, "Okay."

Not much fazed him.

"What time is it?" I asked. "My phone drowned."

He looked at his phone and said, "Five fifteen."

"Shoot, we're late to meet Grandma at the Split Crow. Can I borrow that?"

We stopped walking in front of a used bookstore. He handed me his phone, and I dialed my grandma's number. She picked up on the first ring.

"Evie?" she said in a shout. "Is that you?"

"Yes, Grandma, it's me. I—"

"Where are you? Why aren't you answering your phone? I've been worried sick!"

I pulled the phone back and held it a hand span away from my ear as she blasted me.

"I'm fine, Grandma, and I'm sorry. I just... dropped my phone in a puddle and lost track of time. We'll be there soon." I hung up and handed the phone back to Harold.

"She didn't sound happy," he said. "You could hear her?"

"Loud and clear."

"Well, if she knew the truth, she probably wouldn't give me such a hard time." A series of images flashed through my mind, all the close calls and near misses—a long string of moments that could've killed me throughout the day. "Then again, maybe she'd be even more mad."

"I guess we probably shouldn't tell people what happened," Harold said. "They'd lock us in some asylum and throw away the key."

"Lips sealed," I said with a nod. I took a step, then stopped suddenly.

My blood ran cold, colder than I'd been in the harbor.

"V?" Harold said, looking me up and down. "What is it?"

I pointed a trembling finger at the bookstore's display window.

Harold scanned the window but saw nothing. "What?"

"The book," I said.

"Which one?"

"*That* one!"

A bunch of battered paperbacks and hardcovers were on display. One of them caught my eye.

Haunted Coasts, by Jeremy Alexander Sinclair. The cover showed a creepy lighthouse on the left, an old schooner materializing out of fog on the right, and in the center...

In the center was an illustration of a man. A man I recognized.

A man with long red hair and a bony face.

The man who had broken free of the Wisp's orb, then flown away to who-knows-where.

I entered the shop, grabbed the book, and flipped through the pages. Harold peered nervously over my shoulder.

"Talk to me, V," Harold said with a quiver in his voice. "What's going on?"

"The man on the cover..." My mouth had turned as dry as a desert. I continued to scan the contents of the book. I stopped on a page when I saw another drawing of the man. "He's the same guy I released from the Wisp's orb."

Beneath the illustration was a caption:

Bill the Butcher, the Most Fearsome Ghost of the East Coast

"Harold?" The book nearly slipped out of my fingers. "What have we done?"

© Colleen Morris

Joel A. Sutherland is the author of *Be a Writing Superstar*, numerous volumes of the *Haunted Canada* series (which have received the Silver Birch Award and the Hackmatack Award) and *Frozen Blood*, a horror novel that was nominated for the Bram Stoker Award. His short fiction has appeared in many anthologies and magazines, including Blood Lite II & III and *Cemetery Dance* magazine, alongside the likes of Stephen King and Neil Gaiman. He has been a juror for the John Spray Mystery Award and the Monica Hughes Award for Science Fiction and Fantasy.

He is a Children's & Youth Services Librarian and appeared as "The Barbarian Librarian" on the Canadian edition of the hit television show *Wipeout*, making it all the way to the third round and proving that librarians can be just as tough and wild as anyone else.

Joel lives with his family in southeastern Ontario, where he is always on the lookout for ghosts.

Read all the books in the Haunted series!

HAUNTED

The Nightmare Next Door
Joel A. Sutherland

HAUNTED

Field of Screams
Joel A. Sutherland

HAUNTED

Ghosts Never Die
Joel A. Sutherland

HAUNTED

Night of the Living Dolls
Joel A. Sutherland